When No One's Looking

A Novel
by
Sarah Leamy

Eloquent Books

Copyright © 2010

Eloquent Books
An imprint of Strategic Book Group
P.O. Box 333
Durham CT 06422
www.StrategicBookGroup.com

ISBN: 978-1-60976-243-8

Printed in the United States of America

Book Design: Stacie Tingen

This is a work of fiction. Any resemblance to actual persons, living or
dead, is coincidental.

With Thanks

Much appreciation for Gail Snyder, my editor, for
bringing out the best she could!

And for my family and friends, I thank you for all your love,
laughter and teasing.
You keep asking me if this is an autobiographical novel.
No, of course not, and yes, absolutely.

In memory of my parents. I miss you both.

Chapter One

"You've got to be kidding me. Again?"

Kat nodded.

"You really are telling me this, again? That there is nothing going on between us? No affair? No love?"

I looked into her eyes, as cold and dark as my dog's water was this winter's morning. She watched me. Her arms were folded across her chest as if to protect herself from me. Me. Who has been her sweet secret lover, for how many years now? Five? Ten? More?

Kat forgets.

Like now, when I'm no longer convenient, she forgets how much we have been in each other's lives. How much we mean to each other. She forgets that it's her, always her, who comes back to me, stirs it all up and then leaves once again, usually within a few weeks. She came to me in New Mexico. In Guatemala. In Spain. In Russia. She comes back to me. Always. I don't look for her.

I waited. Kat said nothing. She simply stood there in her leggings and t-shirt. Barefoot, she looked me straight in the eye. Both of us are five foot ten—one of the few ways we are evenly matched.

But then she looked away.

"So, there is nothing going on, right? Why then do you have to shut me out? If there is nothing to hide from Mark, why act as if we're not even friends? Why hide me on the sidelines of your life?"

How I lived with myself, being in the same social circle as this happy couple, I don't know. I didn't look too deeply. I simply wanted her. However I could. Whenever I could.

"Kat. Wake up. Talk to me."

I saw movement in there. She shook loose of her own tight grip. This strikingly dark-haired feline woman shook herself free. Her arms stretched out toward me and then collapsed at her sides.

"Joey. There is nothing going on between us. I told you that last week. I've been nothing but extremely consistent with you about this. There is nothing going on. Now you need to leave. Mark's coming back any minute and I don't want to explain why you're here. He doesn't want you here." She looked at me. "And neither do I."

I watched. I waited. For more. For more honesty. Well, for some honesty. Anything but that dismissal. Sometimes it worked, if I stood and waited. Sometimes she'd remember to reassure me of her deep love, remind me of the passion that sparks and ignites between us when no one's looking. I waited. But no. Not this time. She said nothing else.

I bit my tongue to hold back the bitter words. I tasted the rich blood between my teeth. I wanted to spit it into her mouth, to have her know the depths of how she hurts me with this oh-so-consistent rejection of hers. I didn't. I waited. She folded her arms across her chest again.

That was it, then?

I said nothing more. I turned away, walked to the gate and let myself out, whistling for Jimmy, my Husky mongrel. He bounded up to me. I nodded toward the truck and he sprang into the bed and waited for us to drive off. He watched Kat. I knew it. He adored her, more than a casual friend of mine would usually elicit from this shy dog, but with her—Jimmy was in love.

Chapter Two

Maybe it's my age. I'm seventy-one and counting.

I'm dying. I know it. The doctor knows it. In fact, she tells me to call my closest family to my side, to spend time with me. Now.

"Not for Christmas," says Dr. Nancy, "but now, in November. Thanksgiving is coming up. So invite them over. And anyway, the flights are cheaper!"

She laughs with me, unafraid of my death. Perhaps it's my own lack of fear that opens her up to play and visit as much as she does. Dr. Nan worries for me, being alone up here. Just me and the cats and the dog. I have company, so who's worried?

I am. I worry that my adorable four-legged friends will suffer right after I'm gone. That it will be days before anyone notices. I worry that Nan won't come by for a while, and only then will she find them cold and hungry. I worry that the neighbors won't notice that my truck's not moved or that there is no smoke from the fireplace. Although there is David. He stops by often enough. I haven't told him, though. I haven't told anyone. Maybe I should?

Will I know when I'm about to die? Will I talk to my friends to say goodbye? To ask them to come care for the animals, to feed my babies? Not that they are babies, not now. Two eight-year-old cats and a twelve-year-old lumbering dog named Fred. Not so young for animals. Especially here in New Mexico. Short life expectancy. Like mine. Or is it unlike mine? I didn't expect much, but I kept on living. Until now.

I live in the Ortiz Mountains of Northern New Mexico. In a home I built by hand in my sixties. The other homes of mine have come and gone. Like my ideas of love, of family, even of friendship. Unattached now. I've seen so much come and go, lost so many people I've loved and worshipped. Well, Kat is the only one I worshipped. Such an old-fashioned word, isn't it? Not one people use freely these days. I don't talk about her much nowadays. She was here two years ago. She arrived months after Eleanor died. Kat came here to talk to me. To be with me. Again. Why do I let her keep coming back to me? I don't know. To be truthful, that was the first, and only, time that I sent her packing.

I remember the time I'd needed stitches in my tongue. Well, one stitch. That was painful! She had asked me over to the house I knew so well. We'd stood in the front yard, with the neighbors driving by, waving to the both of us, so familiar were we in this village. We knew the cars, the walks and the affairs of each and every one of the three hundred locals. Kat stood in front of me, arms crossed, telling me to leave her alone. Again. How many times had she said that? By then, we'd been lovers for sixteen years. Sixteen years! Admittedly, not the average type of lovers. An on/off dynamic from day one. A love and hate affair.

And I mean that.

The stitches. I remember walking out of that garden of hers with my jaw so tense that I ached when the doctor finally got me to open up for her to look.

I'd left Kat at her steps. The ones she used to meet me on, half-dressed, starving for my jokes as I tore into her, barely making it back inside the front door. She loved me then. She still does. She forgets. Even now, forty years later, she still forgets. Or is it fifty years? I forget!

I'd left her, calling to my dog, Jimmy. We drove off into Cerrillos, a few miles away, another small town, an ex-mining town, empty but for a petting zoo of chickens, geese and a couple of lamas. I parked next to the Post Office and we walked down the Galisteo basin river. A trickle. No river except in the flash flood seasons of spring and late summer. It was November.

The first frozen night of the year. I'd woken to water bowls solid with ice, and my thirsty dogs. Two of them. One an old-timer who'd stayed home more often than not. Angel came from Paula's family, a bribe to get me to settle down. She was pregnant when she came to live with me. And there was Jimmy, one of her puppies, who was the first dog I raised. Both became company dogs, if you know what I mean.

We walked through the long grasses and Russian olive trees to get to the sand. I didn't cry. I couldn't. My mouth was stuck. So tense I couldn't open it by choice. Not that I wanted to. Not then. I was scared I'd scream. A banshee howl for all the local dogs to join in with. A ripping of the vocal chords to shatter anyone's complacent Saturday morning coffee in bed. Yes, it was early. I remember this all so clearly.

Why do I remember that time? It's not like it was the first or the last time she asked me to leave. And that's what drove me crazy.

The sand was rough to touch. I held it in my left hand and squeezed hard. It gave not an inch. I walked along the flowing streambed. I had to jump across a few deeper spots to save my leather boots from the salty water. High mineral content here in New Mexico. The mines still affect everything, decades later. Did any one learn, though? No. But that's another conversation. That morning, after leaving Kat, I walked and walked. I tried to calm my breathing down, to relax. It was virtually impossible. I was raging. I took off the woolen hat. A present from her three winters before. I didn't throw it away. I shook out my shaggy curly reddish hair, neither long nor short, just about four or five inches of wildness. The cold air attacked my ears, but I didn't care. I stuck my hands back in the pockets of the jacket. My denim jeans, being black, soaked up the bright sunlight. Soon I warmed up. I strode across the dunes, under the golden cottonwoods. Jimmy, all seventy pounds of muscle and fur, came bounding up, with a six-foot tree root in his mouth. He smiled at me and turned and ran, looking

5

back to see if I understood him. I did. I chased him, as he dodged in and out, whacking me with the stick as he passed. I ran and ran. I laughed.

I laughed. Jimmy stopped. He dropped the stick and came back to me. We sat in the sun. He leaned against me, smiling. I laughed again. And noticed the blood splatter onto Jimmy's dusky pepper fur. I put my hand to my mouth. It wouldn't open up for me. Blood dribbled out the corners.

"Make me laugh again, Jimmy," I begged but no words came out. He watched me, and then licked the blood off my hands.

I looked back in the direction of the truck and nodded. Jimmy took off running, and I followed. Slowly. My feet felt far away. How much blood had I swallowed? What had I done to myself this time?

I told myself to look around, to see where I was. Alone, I was alone. The ravens in the tree opposite watched me wobbling back down river. The trees shook more leaves free as another winter storm built momentum. The olives and the cottonwoods, the grasses and the cedars lined the sand banks, shimmering oranges, gold, greens and silver like nowhere else in the world. I stood. I stared. Jimmy came running back, worry written across his canine face. I couldn't reassure him; he was so used to my incessant words that my silence scared him deeply. I held out my right hand to him and he approached me. I stroked his ears and looked into his odd colored eyes, one blue and one amber.

I took a minute to gather my wits about me like a winter coat. I stood up straight. We walked back to the truck. And to the clinic next to it.

Chapter Three

Lisa turned to me. "Do you have an appointment, Joey? I didn't expect you."

She smiled up at me from behind the white tidy counter; her long light brown hair tied up for once. Her soft eyes had a sweetness that melted me. My own eyes watered. This stopped her short.

"Let me go talk to Mary. She usually can fit you in. Take a seat. I'll be right back." She smiled again, this time softer, gentler, as if she knew how my heart broke. My fragile state.

I looked around the clinic. It was empty but for an older woman I knew by sight. She nodded in my direction, then continued reading. In front of her were low metal tables packed with old copies of *Time* and *Oprah* magazines. Three rows of plastic seats, always waiting for more patients. This quiet clinic luckily open every day of the week. Lucky for me, anyways. I walked past her and into the lone unisex bathroom. I wanted to see myself. How did I look to others? How messed up was I?

The bright blue room felt cold to me, not so well-heated as the main room. I took a leak, then washed my hands. November. Flu season. Avoiding that first look at myself. And then, I did it. I looked.

Me. That's me? I was gaunt. Deep shadows around my eyes. They were clouded, shut down. My mouth, though. That's what caught my attention. Splattered with old dried blood. I tried to open my jaw, but I clenched up even more instead. I needed to loosen up. I needed to talk to the nurse, to Mary. Ask her how my tongue was. To tell her I needed help.

I walked back out and was about to take a seat near the front door when Mary came out to get me. She took me along the corridor to the weigh machine. "Just the usual, Joey. Weight. Height. Blood pressure."

I nodded my head but still said nothing.

"Five foot ten. 140 pounds. That's down from last time, isn't it? A bit too low. Blood is low, too. Okay, let's go into the room over there and we can talk."

I grabbed my jacket and followed her inside to sit on the bed. I looked up at her as she read my chart. I'd been coming here for years. Mary knew me. Almost too well. I can't hide from her.

"What are you here for today, then? You don't look so good, Joey. Pale. Shaken. Did something happen?"

I nodded. I opened my mouth.

"Ahh. I see." Mary wasn't shocked. She stepped up closer and looked in my mouth, then reached behind her for the surgical gloves. She held my jaw wide. Vulnerable. I knew her well enough to take it. Her right hand came back out covered in my blood. "Let me get the other nurse and we'll take care of it. It might need a stitch or two. We'll see if we can just pack it down first. Then we need to talk, okay? Okay?"

"Yeah. Okay."

It was all I could manage. But it seemed to encourage her as she smiled briefly before rounding up some extra hands. I waited, my fingers touching my face constantly. Everything was beginning to hurt real bad. Intensely. I had just sat back down when the nurses came in. They took care of it. I held back. Didn't cry out loud, but fuck it hurt. One stitch. Another self-inflicted injury. Nurses don't like that, do they?

Mary left me for five minutes, to gather myself, she said. Then she knocked on the door and let herself back in, smiling at me. Put down my chart, a folder it is by now. "So what happened, Joey? Tell me the whole story. What got you to do that to yourself? I realize that it's not easy to talk. Can you answer some simple questions?" she asked, looking closely at me.

Trying to smile, I nodded.

Mary looked at me again, watched me, and then asked, "Are you sleeping these days?"

"No, not well."

"Is it making you crazy feeling again?"

"Yeah, kinda."

"Manic episodes? Violent? "

"Yeah."

"Do you need more sleeping pills? It's been about six months since the last time."

"Yeah, I need more." I looked away. I hated that I needed help like this. I hated asking for help.

Mary made a note on that day's sheet. "What else? Let's see. Did someone close do something that confused you? Your lover? I know how it gets you when she says one thing and does the opposite."

I nodded my head and the tears began to fall hard and fast. Why was it any tenderness would undo me? I looked away. Mary passed me some tissues. I hated needing them but I did. I wiped up the snot and the blood. I told her about Kat, about the fight/non-fight only hours before, how I'd held back from saying all I wanted. Hence the tongue. The blood. The pain.

Mary listened. She always had been so calm with me. Steady. Solid. "Do you want to hurt yourself?"

"Yeah."

"Are you likely to do something this time?"

"I don't think so. I don't know."

" I think it's time for you to see someone. A professional, someone used to these triggers of yours, someone who knows how to deal with your kind of traumas. I can only patch you up. Will you see a friend of mine in Santa Fe? Dr. Wills. He can listen and help."

I shook my head. I didn't want a psychologist in my head. It's crowded enough in there. Mary talked more, about my kid experiences in the foster homes after mom and dad died, about the patterns she's seen in me over the years, these cycles of mine, the depression that lingers always, ready to overwhelm me once again. And always it comes back to the hospital. Being there for so long. I spent over a year in a psych ward. It's on my record.

"You need help, Joey. More than I can do here."

The tears came again. I couldn't stop them. She left me alone, and filled out the paperwork for the pills. When she came back in, I'd cleaned myself up.

"I'm forty-one," I told her. "And I hate this. It hurts. Too much."

"Good." Mary, big, blond and midwestern in build, gave me a relieved look, then handed me the bottle of pills. "One at night. It will help you fall asleep. That will help your moods. Are you eating enough?"

"Enough? Well, what I have, what I can."

"Come back in two weeks. I want to check your mouth and your weight. Get more food. Promise me?"

"Yeah, I promise."

"Good. Then come back in two weeks. Take care of yourself, Joey. Eat. Sleep. Call the doctor at this number."

Chapter Four

David, my best friend's grandson, comes over with a truckload of pi-ñon and juniper. He throws it all near my front door and then pulls out his chainsaw. "I found this wood on the side of the road. Thought you might like it, Joey. Can you use it?"

David is six-foot-two with a reddish-brown ponytail tied back, and he is strong, young and tireless. He's building a straw-bale home for himself up the road from mine, drives by every evening after spending his days working in Santa Fe. He usually waves from the big red Ford truck as he passes. I spend my afternoons on the front steps to my cabin. He's a good kid. Not a kid, really. Mid-twenties. So young to my eyes, but still. He's his own person now, a good and steady young man.

"Thanks, David. What do I owe you this time?"

"Ahh, nothing. You know me. A good story and a beer after work is enough. Did you get any of that Green Chile beer? I liked that stuff."

I climb out of the rocking chair and head into the kitchen. My knees ache but I'm still pretty mobile. You'd never guess my time is running out. David doesn't know yet. The cooler is full of beer for my helpful friends. I come back and sit in the sunny spot, open the beers and offer him one.

"Let me cut some of this up first. Then we can catch up, OK?" David pulls on his helmet, straps on the chaps and fires up the saw. He's so sen-sible. I used to wear my cowboy hat and sunglasses when I bucked wood for myself. It seemed enough to me. Kept sawdust out of my eyes, that was my main concern. Oh, I wore steel capped boots. There you go, I was careful, right?

I watch David. It's hard to watch. Watch and do nothing. I always did everything myself. It drove my lovers crazy that I couldn't ask for help. I did it, though, made a home or four, over the years. My first place was when I was David's age. Mid-twenties.

I had come to New Mexico on my way to California, then on to Old Mexico. That had been the plan. I bumped into a few casual new friends at some bar in Santa Fe.

One of them, a unique, slender, funky artist type, with almost black straight shoulder length hair, charcoal grey eyes and a wide smile, chatted to me about the wood sculptures she was creating, and then asked me about myself. I told her little to start with. Traveling. Stuff like that. Vague. I tended to keep quiet and ask the questions, not the other way around. She stood as tall as me, with those uniquely grey eyes that stared far into me as she spoke. I nervously looked around for a distraction. The band started up. Country and Western. Perfect for this cowboy joint.

"Come dance with me, Kat."

I looked over to the empty wooden floor to our left. She looked at me as if studying my intentions, then laughed out loud. Sudden and bright, her laughter rocked into me. I was smitten. That deeply freeing laugh of hers caught me and I looked back at her. A wicked grin escaped from behind her glass in hand. She knew. She knew. She saw who I was beneath these worn out clothes of mine. With that perceptive look she gave me, she caught hold of me.

" I don't know how to follow. I usually lead," she finally answered the question.

I reached out my hand to her and she took it. "Trust me, you'll follow me just fine."

It was the first time we'd touched. I forgot her name. My own name. I forgot where I was. The sexual charge took us both by surprise. Frozen in place for a second too long. Then the rhythm woke me up and I stepped out with her hand in mine. Self-conscious, yet in charge. She'd probably deny it and say she was playing with me that first night. Such was the dynamic between us from day one.

We danced for most of the night. Other friends tried to cut in, to dance with her, sometimes to dance with me. But we kept coming back, reaching for each other instinctively. Losing all sense of those around us. She followed well, fitting into my body, finding my rhythm, relaxing and staring and laughing with me. We danced. Talked. Forgot. Got lost. In each other.

"Hey, Joey! You napping while I work? Is that it?" David's question brought me back to the cooling afternoon sunshine. My beer was half-empty. David stood next to a huge pile of cut wood, with his arms full of yet more for inside.

"Were you thinking of Kat? You had that look you get."

"Yeah, I remembered my first night in town, meeting her, dancing all night till the bar closed down."

David smiles at me, knowing the story—well, some of the story. He loves to share his growing adventures of lovers he's had so far, and finds it amazing that I still inspire love and hate in Kat. He happened to be here one time when she showed up out of the blue. He's witnessed the chemistry between us. David grins as he steps over the sleeping dog and carries the wood inside.

"Hey, you been tidying up? You expecting visitors? Or was this for me? Did my mom tell you I was coming over?"

"Ha. Ha. No, I like it tidy—you should know that."

"But this is clean, not just tidy!"

"Get out here and drink your beer. Don't you be worrying about my social life!"

David closes the big wooden door behind him. "I put some kindling on the ashes, so the fire should kick back in for you. I didn't mean to pry. Mom's been worried about you, that's all. So I end up worrying."

I pass him a beer and we watch each other. For one so young, David takes me by surprise at how much he notices and cares. Not sure I did when I was his age. I smile. "No harm. And yeah, I have a feeling I'm going to have visitors soon."

"How come?"

I shake my head, no answer. "It's just a feeling. And well, it *is* the season, right?"

We sit back in the rocking chairs, ones we painted together quite a few winters back. He'd been given them by a client who'd thought they were too old for her Eldorado home. He brought them over here one weekend. We sanded them, and then painted one blue and one pink. It makes him laugh each time I choose to sit in the pink one. For that alone, I do it. He knows I don't like pink. Never have.

The sun is beginning to set already; five pm and it's getting dark. The clocks turned back last Sunday. I am still getting used to it.

David is quiet. He has something on his mind. I can tell. He needs to talk.

I wait. Happy in my home. The critters lie around in the warm spots next to us. David pulls out a pipe.

"Want some?"

"Your own?"

He nods and passes it to me to smell. Fresh and potent. "I like that. Smells fine to me! Don't tell your mom, though. She thinks I'm a bad influence as it is."

"You wish! Maybe when I was a teenager spending all my time up here. Now she thinks I'm the bad influence on *you*!" David laughs and takes his time, packing the pipe, lighting it up for me and watching my deep breaths. He sits back after a few minutes. "Can I ask you something?"

"Of course. Is it a girl?"

"I think she'd want to be called a woman, but yeah, it is. I don't know what to do, Joey."

"Is it Jamie? The one you talk about all the time? What happened?" I lean down to scratch Fred's ears. He's mostly deaf but he likes to listen in to the two of us, sitting as close as he can get. Fred sighs. David sighs. I wait.

I wait easily nowadays. Finally patience finds me at home. Manic no more. Depressed no more. Thankfully, for me. In a lifetime of hyper-activity, anger filled my marrow and leaked out whenever I wasn't looking. Now I wait for David to tell me his woes. Patiently. We talk easily, honestly. I like this kid. He's like my own family, and if I'd had any, I hope we would've been friends like this. But no kids for me. I'd spent too many years wandering around, getting closer to Kat and then leaving fast, heading far away whenever we crashed into the walls that hid us. And we always did, eventually.

David finishes the first beer and heads in to grab us another each. I hear him tend the woodstove. He comes back out. "I don't know what to do this time. Jamie called me, invited me over, we had a great time and then she told me the next morning that she can't be with me. It's that fast. One minute she's there, and the next she's not. Gone. Gone and gone. It's driving me crazy."

I open the beers and hand him one. "You know my track record! I can't give you any advice, David. I don't know how to be with anyone. I don't know why Eleanor stayed with me! Fifteen or so years, that's true, but I sure don't understand relationships, not really."

"Me, neither."

"What do you want? Can you tell her?" I make it sound so easy, don't I? Just talk to her. Right. It doesn't work that way. I talked so much. It didn't help. Usually dug me further into the pits. Eleanor didn't ask me to talk. She just took me as I am.

David sips the beer. "She's cut me off. I have to wait till she calls me. I don't want to wait for her, but I'm so into her, I can't focus on anyone else. You know the feeling, don't you? Like those stories you told me about Kat, when you first met her."

Yeah. Like when I first met her. Kat.

Chapter Five

"Maker's Mark."

"What?"

"Maker's Mark," Kat repeated.

"What's that?"

Kat laughed again. "That's what I drink."

"Oh! Right! I'll go get you a drink." I came back a minute later. "How do you like it?"

"Straight up. No ice. And thanks, Joey." She looked down, and then stared back into me with a slightly shy smile. It was the first time she looked a little uncertain. More vulnerable.

Kat was so beautiful to me that night. Radiant somehow. I wandered off to the bar and got our drinks. Another ale for me. Maker's Mark for her. I walked back to where I'd left her but didn't see her. I found a wall to lean against by the back door. I kept looking around. I stood there, suddenly uncertain myself. Had she gone? I just stood there for a while. Then I found her. Saw her, that is. Kat stood near the kitchen door, deep in conversation with another woman, small, dark and stocky. Their body language held me away, with Kat half backing off from the other woman, yet she acted tense and proud at the same time. I waited and sipped my beer. What to do. What to do.

"Sorry about that. That was my ex."

"Oh. Er. So you like girls?" I passed her the whiskey.

She drank deeply, savoring the taste before she answered me. "I like girls. I like boys." She watched me as I took this in.

"That's good, then. An equal opportunity lover."

"Not quite, but we can talk about that another time. Come on, Joey, let's go outside."

Kat finished her drink and held out her hand for mine. I put my beer down and followed her, instinctively looking up as we passed the kitchen. Her ex-girlfriend stared at me. I looked back. And I held on to Kat. I couldn't do anything but follow.

"Let's sit over there," she suggested and we crossed the road to the low adobe wall. Under the tree we sat, facing each other. Silent. Finally silent. The noise and the chaos of the bar left us and we were alone. Just Kat and me. How many hours had passed since we first chatted? It felt late. It was late. Like I said, I was smitten. Oblivious.

"Tell me a story." Kat wanted more stories, and then more stories from other places around the country. I was flattered, I admit it.

I looked up at the stars above Santa Fe. I paused, wondering which one to mention. What did I want her to know about me? "I first visited New Mexico a few years ago. I've been traveling back and forth since then, mostly working festivals, writing, taking photos. That kind of thing. I was trying my hand at writing some articles. And then last winter, I went back to Maine. I'd planned on going back to college, starting a degree in journalism. I'd turned twenty-five, figured it was time to do the right thing, you know?"

Kat nodded but said nothing.

"But I couldn't do it. I tried. I found a place, moved in, made myself a home, built a social life again through working at the market around the corner from my place."

"Where were you?"

"In Portland. The college was way across the city. I took my bike every morning. I liked the teachers enough. The school was pretty up-to-date, too. I liked it. I just couldn't do it. Couldn't fit in like that. Not for me. I left." That was the abbreviated form of the last major life change. Not a full story but a hint. I didn't know how much she wanted to hear. I waited.

"You left the school? Or Maine?"

"Both. The college culture, the pace of living there, it was too much for me. I missed the freedom of not knowing where I'd be sleeping each night. Not knowing where I'm going next. Life on the edge, in a sense. Living in my home state kept me too safe, too boxed in. So, well, now I'm back on the road. Footloose, kinda. And you? Want to tell me anything?"

Kat still held my left hand and she absently played with my fingers as she stared off watching her friends leave the bar. "Last call, I guess," she said.

"Yeah, it has that late night feel."

"Do you miss your family?"

"No. I don't really have one. I should feel bad about saying that out loud. But no. We're not really family. Not close. More like landlords and me the unwanted tenant. Too much trouble for them, they can't take the questions from the neighbors." I looked at her. And before she could ask what I meant, I blurted out, "Can I take you home, Kat? Spend the night with you?"

She leaned in and kissed me. A passing kiss, a drive-by. Then she watched me and kissed me again. Time enough for the both of us to know this was a kiss of promise, desire and a deep knowing passion. Special, there was some special attraction and understanding between us. Her lips pulled me in further and she explored mine with her tongue. And then she sat back, sat quietly.

I waited. "You didn't answer my question," I reminded her softly.

"No, I didn't. Well, maybe," she looked up with a wide wicked grin, "maybe I did in a way! But, no, I can't invite you back." Kat shivered.

I pulled her against me and wrapped her up in my arms, waiting to hear more. Her hair tickled me and I brushed it to the side. She wore a pink skirt over her jeans, with black and red cowboy boots, and some kind of short black t-shirt clinging to her upper body. She had some pretty obvious muscles and was definitely fit from sculpting. I held her against me. I breathed in deeply. Kissed her shoulder and felt her shiver. "Why can't I come back with you? I can give you a ride if you want. That's my motorcycle over there." I pointed out the old blue Honda with luggage strapped to the sides and back seat.

"That's yours? Did you just get here?"

"Yeah, a few hours before I met you here. On my way to some friends of mine in San Francisco. In a roundabout kind of way, that is. Want to come with me?"

"Yes!" Kat laughed. But I had a feeling something else was going on for her. "But I can't. And anyway, you don't know me! Do you always ask women to come with you?"

I couldn't help but grin. "Right. It looks like I have space for another body on that, does it? I mean, I could make space to take you home," I reminded her, "but no, you're the first I've asked!"

Kat laughed and sat back up and out of my arms. She kissed me again, this time softly, distantly, as if she was leaving me already.

"Well, now what?" I asked.

"Not much. I stay. You go."

"Not necessarily. We both stay. We both go? Take your pick."

Kat changed the subject, almost, and asked where was I planning on staying that night. I described Paula's cabin south of town, how I can stay with her for a while. "It's five miles up a county road, a dirt road up into the mountain. The cabin itself is small, woodstove, rainwater and all of that. It sounds pretty sweet to me. I haven't experienced anything like that yet.

My only fear is getting there. I hope the road's not too rough for me. My balance with all that stuff on the motorcycle is, well, is a little off."

"What have you got on there?" She sounded honestly curious, and happier to be on safer ground with me.

"Well, I'd been living with someone in Madison, and so I had all this stuff. Settling down does that, accumulates, stuff accumulates around me. Anyway, I gave a bunch away when we ended whatever it was we had. That was a few months ago. And so I just gathered up all the basics and headed southwest. So, I have tent, a great sleeping bag, a change of clothes, some spare bike parts, and a teddy bear named Oliver."

"You like traveling on your own?" She was shocked. "I'm never alone, always had someone beside me."

"Yeah, I love it, the complete freedom and openness to new folks. There's nothing between me and them, so how can they treat me with anything but openness, too? But, well, I can tell you about that later tonight!" I was relentless, trying to get her to spend the night with me. Or me with her.

Kat stood up, though, and shook herself quickly. I kissed her. Time was running out; I felt her slide away from me. I was right. Next thing she said was, "I want more, but I can't." She stepped back from me.

"Why not?" I asked.

Her eyes looked sad to me. "Because I live with my ex. And it's too new; she doesn't know how over it is. She still thinks we're together."

"Are you? Together still?"

"In a sense, yes. The house, the dogs, we work together. Yes, it's complicated."

I looked around, and noticed that the bar was closing down for the night. The last few cars drove by. I felt alone. Kat waited for me to say something. But what could I say? So you're still with her? Then why kiss me? Why all this attention when you can't be with me? Why pull me in and then say you have to go? That I have to go?

I said nothing.

"Like I said, I want more but I can't. I'm sorry, Joey. Look, I should go."

"Do you need a ride?" I asked out of habit. But I didn't want to return her to a home she shared with another. Just being polite.

Kat shook her head quickly. "No. But thanks. Are you going out West tomorrow? Keep on driving? Leave?"

"I don't know. I really don't know what I'm doing next." My voice sounded so quiet now. Kat leaned in and gave me one last gentle kiss.

"Well, goodbye, Joey. Take care of yourself. Okay?"

"Yeah, okay. You too. I had a beautiful night with you. Don't forget."

"I won't," and she walked away. She crossed Guadalupe Street and climbed into a sweet-looking white Land Rover and then drove off. She looked over as she passed by.

I sat on the wall.

"Don't forget," I said to myself.

Chapter Six

"Is that why you stayed then? For Kat?" David sits forward in his chair, tapping out the pipe, curious to find out more. More about my arrival here in New Mexico and my travels before settling into these hills in the late '60s. Some forty years ago now. Oh, my God, that's a long, long time! Hah.

"Yes. No. Not really. Haven't I ever told you this before? I forget. Not sure what I've told you."

David looks at me. "Yeah, you've told me, but I like the story. And anyway, are you okay? You don't usually say stuff like that. If you're tired, I can come back tomorrow."

"No, I'm fine, a little forgetful about the last few days. Can't remember who I've talked to. Nothing to worry about though. Where was I?"

David looks uncertain, but he reminds me of the story of my meeting Kat.

"My twenties! So long ago. I had fun, I must admit. Are you, David, having fun?"

He grins widely. "Oh yeah, sure am. Can't be beat! Even with girl stuff getting me down, it doesn't keep me down, you know?"

"Yeah, I can see that. It didn't mess me up then, either. It was later, in my thirties and forties, that I didn't do so well. But that's a whole other story…"

I drift for a second, nowhere specific but quiet. David, too.

Fred lumbers to his feet and faces the front door. The wind is picking up and the temperature drops suddenly.

"Want to come in for supper? I made a green chile stew. There's more than enough to share."

23

"I'd love some. I can't stay long; it's been a tiring day at work. I'm ready to sleep, but the sound of some hot stew is too good. Thanks."

Inside, David tends the fire. I put the saucepan on the woodstove and then feed the cats and of course Fred gets his bowl of food. The animals settle in for the night. I look around the cabin, the homestead. Not so much just a cabin anymore but it's simple, rustic I guess. A straw-bale home with saltillo tiled floors, mud plaster and a four-poster bed tucked into the far corner. The shower is open to the room with beautiful blue and green tile work. The kitchen has a square wooden table taking center stage. Four chairs—why four, I don't know. I never need four.

"Maybe I will, though."

"Will what?"

"Oh. Thinking out loud. I was just wondering why I have four chairs and how maybe I'll use them all at once sometime soon."

"Hey, that's the second time you've mentioned or hinted that you've got people coming. What's up?"

David brings over two big blue bowls and ladles out our supper. He passes one to me and then sits down next to the stove, in the second beat-up armchair. I'm curled up in my favorite one, the green corduroy one.

"I don't know. I just have a feeling that I'm going to get busy here. I might go into town tomorrow and pick up some supplies for us. Do I need more beer?"

"Probably. Want me to pick some up, even though you're not telling me anything?"

I eat my food. David eats. Fred eats. The cats are done first.

"I can't say yet, David. No offense. But I kinda think your Uncle Mike might show up soon. Some other old friends of mine from many years ago. I'll have to tell you about them before then. And. Well. Kat, too. I think she'll be here. It's like there's something shifting and I need to prepare for it." I simply can't explain to him that time, the concept of my limited time, is leaving me restless and yet calm. Time. Not many tomorrows for me.

"Kat shows up every so often. You know that. Since I've been thinking about her so much, she might be thinking of me, too. Corny, I know, but! heh, I've always been a romantic."

"You have? I can't see you that way. I think of you as practical, grounded somehow."

I laugh. Stew flies. "Me? Grounded? Well, *now*, maybe, but sometime soon I'll tell you about all the craziness I done all over this damn country. And in other countries, too. I messed up big time in the '80s. Not a good example for you, so don't remind your mom, okay? There's a reason I had to settle here! I burned too many bridges. I couldn't go back to Moscow, for example."

"Who'd want to go back there?"

I chuckle and he laughs as I clean up the mess I made. Fred helps where he can. David takes the bowls to the sink for me. He checks to see that I'm okay for wood for the night, then gives me a quick hug. That's new. I hug him. And then he leaves. My eyes tear up. My boy. My friend. My friends.

Chapter Seven

I sat on the wall for a while, surprised at myself for feeling so blue without Kat next to me. We'd talked so much about the creative stuff of life. It hadn't occurred to me that she might be with someone, not be free like me. I'd been sure she wanted me as much as I did her. Bummer, huh? Oh well. I stood up and crossed the road and took out the bike keys. Time to go. Time to go find Paula.

Paula and I had met in Chicago in the early '60s, a few years ago. We were both twenty at the time. She was a Scot, and had been visiting the U.S. when she fell in love and settled, first in the Midwest and then she and her new husband Chris moved to New Mexico, of all places. His home state. They now had three kids and were living the hippy lifestyle full on.

Paula and I knew each other pretty well, considering how little time we'd spent together. I was happy for her—the bare-foot and pregnant thing worked for her. And whenever we got to talk, it all just flowed. In-depth conversations about life, the great writers, taking it slow in the mountains, and whatever made us both laugh until we snorted out loud. She was becoming like a sister to me.

And I knew that I could ask her about Kat. Maybe Paula knew the story? Knew the couple? It was a small town, Santa Fe, back in those days, maybe twenty thousand, if that. So she might know the background that Kat hadn't offered herself. Yet. And yeah, I knew Paula would tease me bad, but it'd be worth it, just to find out more. Was Kat really breaking up with her girlfriend? Did I have a chance? That's what it boiled down to: Did I have a chance?

Should I stay? Or should I go?

Red or green? Stop or go?

The bike took me up County Road 55, up toward the Ortiz Mountains. The directions were straightforward and I found the driveway easily after driving for three miles up a gravel and rough dirt road. I pulled the bike up behind a red Toyota pick-up. Tired. The drive had been slippery the last stretch, and I'd fallen once. As to picking up the bike with all my stuff—pure adrenalin, nothing else worked. No one around to help me, right? This was my introduction to rural New Mexico. And anyway, if not me, then what else could I have done? Left the bike in the middle of the track? No.

Heavy but do-able. I picked it up and drove to Paula's. Drove the last little bit to the cabin and, like I said, parked. I took the helmet off, took the leathers off and stared at my worldly belongings.

And then I sat down.

What did I see? Just mountains, tons of piñon and juniper, long dirt roads and a shit load of stars. Nothing more. Or less. So empty. It took my breath away, so I rolled a cigarette from the pack. Time to smoke. Keep me grounded before I embarrassed myself in front of Paula. She was expecting me to get there this afternoon. It was midnight now. Oh well. I'd be staying in the cabin next to hers. If a light were on, I'd go knocking. That was my plan. Smoke. Walk. Talk. Perfect.

I pulled out my sleeping bag and a flashlight and followed the gravel path uphill. Not bad. So damn quiet, though. Not sure I could live this far out of town, away from people. I found the little shack Paula said was ready for me. I saw it. A ten or twelve foot rectangle of wood and adobe bricks with a little chimney sticking out the top. Smoke drifted out in the moonlight. The door opened up to one room with a big double bed, a small wooden table and an armchair next to the woodstove. A note lay propped on the pillow for me: "Welcome home, Joey! Do what you like —except for waking the kids and me. It's been hard enough to get them to sleep and having you here will just stir up Maggie all over again. I'll bring you coffee in the morning. Sleep well, friend!"

Shame. I'd hoped to talk to her. It could wait, though. Just girl stuff—I didn't want to make this into a big deal.

I shook out my sleeping bag and set in onto the bed. Extra layers can't be bad. It had gotten cold out there the last few days. A cold spring night in New Mexico. And why not? The view from the deck was inspiring in its barrenness. A full metal dish of hot water sat on the top of the woodstove. I washed out the long day; five hours riding the bike to get out of Colorado, and then the roller coaster of meeting a stranger who'd caught my attention so quickly and, well, so deeply.

I washed her off me. The taste of her on my lips, on my hands. All gone.

Who was I trying to kid? She was still with me.

I sat on the bed after stoking the fire with the mixed wood next to it. Paula had truly made a home here. And I loved it all: the acrylic paintings on the walls, the homemade afghan blanket wrapped across my legs, the table–even that had the hand-hewn feel to it. The white candles, I bet Paula had made those, too.

What a perfect den this place was. If only Kat had come back with me, I'd be exploring every inch of her under the flickering lights, our words mixing with the sounds of the fire, her scent intertwining with the smells of the woods surrounding our cabin. With me. I craved her with me.

I lay there and fell asleep imagining her with me. With me.

Kat. Come home with me. Please.

Chapter Eight

"Joey! Joey! Wake up! Wake up! Mama has coffee for you but you gotta come wiv me. Honest! Honest! I'm not lying. I'm not. Coffee is ready. Now! Now! Now!"

Maggie, three years old and hyper, came rushing in, full of words and bouncing on the bed, startling me out of the sweetly longing dreams of mine, waking me to her huge kid smile.

"Look at my picture. That's me. I did that for you." And she unfolded a pink paper with a painting of a blue and red squiggle; lucky she'd said what it was. I'd have had no idea, otherwise.

I took the paper from her and looked carefully at it and then at her. She stood for me. Waited. Wriggled but still she waited for me to say something about it.

"You look great, Maggie. And I love the picture. It's perfect. Let's put in on the wall with your mama's, okay? And did you promise me coffee?"

"Yeah." Maggie nodded and her shoulder length red hair flopped all over the place. She was wearing her brother's hand-me-downs, with the purple bibs turned up to stop her tripping too easily. The striped orange and grey long-sleeved shirt was coming untucked. Charming. This girl stole my heart every time I saw her.

I climbed out from under the sheets and woolen blankets, still in my well-worn blue jeans and stripy green shirt. No boots, though, just black smelly socks.

"Hey, you didn't wear pajamas! I'm telling Mama. She makes me put on Mikey's pajamas but I don't like them. They're horrible. They smell like him. Joey? Why? Why do you sleep in them dirty jeans?"

I didn't really have an answer so I grabbed her and flung her across my shoulders. Maggie squealed in pure glee. I ran across the yard to the open door, yelling like a banshee.

Paula stepped aside as we ran around the kitchen table before I threw my little monkey into a chair at the breakfast table. The boys beamed and laughed and yelled. All in the same breath. Paula watched us and poured me coffee as I settled them all down again. Well, I tried to. Mikey, the middle child at four-and-a-half, was the shyest, but he gave me the speediest hug, as if I might not notice if he ran past me fast enough. He was another redhead like his mama, this time with green eyes and pale skin. The oldest fella, Charlie, had his father's dark-skinned good looks; even at six you could sense it in him, he'd be a striking young man soon. And already he was tanned by all the time spent outdoors.

I sat down.

Finally Paula had a chance to speak. "Well? Where were you last night, Joey? We made you a special dinner, didn't we?"

The kids all shook their heads. "No, you made it Mama, not us. We just ate it."

"You in trouble!" shouted little Maggie.

Paula looked serious for all of two seconds, and then she laughed. She grinned at me. "Got you! Well, I had to pretend, right? You were so late getting here. Not that you could've called. No phone around here. Just in town. Anyway, still take your coffee black? A little honey?"

"Sounds perfect to me. And what's for breakfast? Can I make a special request? Scrambled eggs with bacon and toast!"

Paula flung the spoon at me. The kids squealed. I threw it back at her. Hit her, too. Yeah, sassy, I know, but that's how it was with us. Family. No matter how long between visits. The sister I'd never wanted until now.

Oats and honey, followed by coffee and more coffee. That's what I got. Like the rest of them. The lightness and playfulness was such a tonic for me. I'd had a rough night's sleep. Restless legs kicked me out of those dreams of an unattainable woman. And my will power couldn't fight that damn fantasy from reaching deep into every minute I slept.

The night had drained me.

Now, though, well, the kids showed me stuff they'd made with the sticks and rocks they'd found and then painted. They finished eating and ran outside to play with the dog, Angel.

Paula sighed. She sat down at the table and pulled the honey jar to her. Finally a mug of coffee for her, too. We sat in the quiet for a while. It felt so good to be here with her and her kids. Chris wasn't around. Instead of asking about it, I enjoyed the time for just the two of us. I heard the boys run past, yelling for Maggie to chase them. Paula smiled to herself as she sipped her drink.

"Well, how are you, Paula? You look great, tired but happy, if you know what I mean. This suits you, huh?"

Paula looked up at the home she and Chris had created together in the last two years. A home full of the clutter of kids and animals and artwork and woodwork and so many beautifully crafted bits and bobs of furniture. We caught each other's eyes and laughed.

"Who'd have thought it?"

Paula shook her head and laughed again. "Yes, this suits me, for sure. The kids are wonderful. Chris and I are doing pretty well. We had a rough patch after Maggie came along, but that's better. Living here is good for all of us. You should join us! The kids love you. You could be my live-in nanny! We could make a right girl out of you!"

"Ha Ha. Not funny." I frowned and Paula laughed out loud again.

"Nanny Joey! Oh, I love it!"

31

"Don't you be using that name, missy. I'll get you back. I'll tell the boys about how you used to chase the boys in Chicago across the lakefront, trying to grab them to see if anything would fall off if you yanked hard enough! You terrified them all! Well, except Chris, I guess!"

Paula threw the spoon at me again. It missed and fell into the plant pot. Pot plant. "Ah. You really do have a green finger. You got more stashed around here?"

"Maybe! You still smoking and toking, Joey? We hope to grow enough to pay off the land in the next year or so. It doesn't cost much to buy a good size acreage of mountainside, if you wanted to settle down near us. We'll be home free in two or three years, I hope. We grow all year 'round, so it's a good income. Chris's wonderful with plants. I never knew! Most of our own food comes from his gardens. I'll let him show you himself when he gets back."

"Where is he? I was going to ask, but, well, I never know how to ask stuff like that in case it's something shitty. So, Chris? Where? By the way, I've had way too much coffee, I'll be following you and talking to you like Maggie does, all the time, right? See? See? I'm already doing it! Chris! Where is he?"

Paula took my mug from my hands and set it down on the counter behind her. She told me how he'd driven south to meet another grower in Las Cruces, to see how he did the selling side of things. "It's kinda risky, but Madrid's a ghost town. We're about five miles away once you get on the highway again. Twenty minutes or so. No one lives out here. So there's no one around. It's really quiet out here. We want to make a more solid greenhouse at some point, for food and the rest of it. I'd like chickens. One thing at a time. Kids first. Now I have more energy for the other stuff. And Chris seems to, as well."

Paula got up and got us both some water from the jug by the back door. She looked outside and saw all three with hands in the compost pile, squealing with whatever they'd pulled out. She closed the door. "I heard it might snow tonight. Should we cover your bike? How long you want to stay this time?"

"Ah, well, I'm not sure, really. I'd planned to ride out to California to hang out with Tom and his sister. I looked forward to the ride through the desert."

"You've been there before— didn't you go there a few years ago?"

"No. Never made it. I might not this time, either. I kinda wanted to talk to you about this. Being in limbo-land again. Too many great choices! Girls. Sunshine. Festivals. Friends. How do I choose?"

Paula took me seriously. "You'll know. You'll know when you meet the one you want to settle with. I honestly believe that, Joey. That's the only big choice you need to make. Or notice, perhaps? The rest? It's just choices."

I stood up. Stretched. "Where's the outhouse? And then I'll tell you about last night, among some other good stories!"

She pointed me downhill and to the left. Luckily, Maggie didn't notice me walk past. She would've followed me, chatting as I sat in the outhouse, asking me why, why and why.

Chapter Nine

"I think I met her. The one I want. But. Well. It's complicated. Like she told me, it's complicated."

Paula was so taken aback that she simply stared at me. Not one joke. Nothing. Stared at me like I was some freak show.

"You can speak still, right?" I prodded.

Paula sat down on the steps next to me. The kids were still running past us every so often, but totally focused on their own adventures. We sat in the morning sun.

"I've never known this kind of sunshine before. It was different in the Midwest. The altitude, maybe." I gave her time to come back to earth. I glanced over to find her staring at me; shock was lingering in her expression. "What? Thought I'd never find someone? Or that I wouldn't tell you?"

"No. Just, well, surprised, I guess. When? Who? Tell me everything!"

I rolled a smoke for myself and lit up. I stared at the mountains in front of us. "What are they called?"

"The Sangre de Cristos. But don't change the subject. Talk to me. Right now!"

I looked up at the blue sky, only a handful of clouds to the south of us. Paula nudged me. "Okay. Okay. I know you'll give me shit, but here goes. Last night I stopped at the bar on Guadalupe, bumped into some familiar faces. And a new face, too. Kat. Kat Buckman."

"Kat Buckman? Are you sure? Funky, intelligent, creative? And striking to look at, not pretty but most definitely striking, yes, that's Kaitlin Buckman."

"Do you know her? Her story?"

Paula shook her head. "Not really. I know she lives halfway between here and Santa Fe, in the old Lone Butte community, a long-lasting ranching area. Her girlfriend's family is from around there; they have a home and studio, lots of great parties there in the summer. What else? Kat's kind of new to town, about three or so years, like us, I guess. Seems crazy but in a good way. A bit of a charmer if she wants something. Well, that's my impression. She talked to Chris but ignored me. Wanted to score from him. Anyway, she seemed pretty friendly. Funny, too. Smart. Yeah, I can see why you'd like her. I could imagine you two together."

I pulled out the tobacco and rolled a smoke. Offered Paula one but she'd gone all healthy since the kids came along. I lit up and waited for more. Nothing came, though.

"Paula? How come you're not asking me all those questions you throw at me when I say I met someone?"

"This feels different to me. You feel different to me. Solid. Like you really know. I can't explain it. It's in your eyes, too. Softer yet clear. That's not like you!"

"Hey, now! Be nice to me," I joked.

"That's what I mean, I feel like I need to be gentle with you." She sighed and reached over and took a drag on the smoke. "So how can I help you? What do you need?"

"I don't know. I was hoping you'd tell me what to do. What next."

" Do you want to meet her again?"

"Absolutely! But I don't know how to find her. She didn't say."

"I can show you her place later. We need to drive into town to get some supplies. Want to come along with us? For the drive? We go past her place. Theirs, I guess. I can also show you where they hang out. But it's always the two of them."

"I met the girlfriend. Well, I saw her, small with intense energy. She stared at me, but I didn't get it at the time. Now I do. Ah, shit. What have I done to myself this time?"

I put the cigarette out and tore up the last bit of paper and scattered it into the dirt at my feet. "Hey, Paula. Do you think I have a chance?"

"I have no idea. But you need to find out, right? Let's go past her place this afternoon, and you can go back tomorrow and talk to her, see if you can hang out together. That's all I can think of. See if it's really there."

"It is. I can't sleep."

Chapter Ten

I wake up to a cold cabin. Fred has jumped onto my bed and is snoring like the little lamb he isn't. Both cats, I forget names more nowadays so I call them both Kit-Kit. It doesn't matter which. Either works. Anyway, one of them is curled up on my lap, the other on my hat. The hat is on the floor next to the bed, not on my head.

I watch my four-legged friends sleeping deeply. It can be so amazingly quiet in here. It still surprises me, even after four decades spent in New Mexico, the amount of silence to be found in one mountain range. Fred stirs and sees me awake. He looks momentarily guilty for some reason. I smile. He lays his head back down. My sweet boy. Fred is a golden retriever and collie mix. I loved my mutts. All were lovely company. I couldn't imagine a life without them. Yeah, well. Right here. Right now. That's the philosophy, right?

I studied Zen Buddhism in my fifties, when I lived in a small fishing village in Wales. I still try to practice the walking meditation when I stroll my land here. Meditation calmed me down. Almost said medicine. It *is* like medicine, to me. Did me more good than the drugs the head-doctor gave me. For those panic attacks, rage and the depressions. I've said it before and I'll keep on saying it: Buddhism is like therapy, only cheaper.

I walk slowly across to the bed, kicking off my leather work boots on the way. I ignore the cooling woodstove. It's warm enough under the covers. I'll be just fine.

Sleep comes easily these days.

Dr. Nan says that the tumor will spread. She says I could take care of it with surgery, chemo and all that. I can't afford it. Actually, I don't want it. Hospitals. All of that.

I'm thinking to just take my sweet time here, at home. Four months isn't much time, though. I suppose there's no point pretending to my friends. It's going to be obvious in the next couple of months. Inevitable.

I'd like to tell people. Tell Paula. Tell her what's been going on. I just never learned how to say stuff. Not really. I shouted, I lied or I left.

When I wake again, the sun is creeping across my feet. Must be six in the morning. Kit-Kit, one and two, jump up once they know I'm awake. They come sit near my face and purr as they hope for some of my loving, followed by some breakfast. I sit up and lean against the wall. Number one cat, the boy, crawls onto my lap. He doesn't ask for much, but with a big yawn and chesty rattle, how can I resist those green eyes? I rub that soft belly of his. The cats are Russian Blue siblings. Identical. Hence the names. Well, identical but for one has a penis and the other doesn't.

Fred sleeps on. I climb out of the blankets and throw on the robe and head outside to take the first leak of the day. I greet my mornings in style, I must say. I look out at the Sangre de Cristo Mountains to the north of me. Snow tops the Baldy peak even though that's earlier than usual. I notice how David had brought me a huge pile of piñon. I hadn't appreciated how big a load his truck carried. I'll have to make him something special.

Or maybe I have something in the trunk? Yeah, I'll pull it out later and see what grabs my eye. A keepsake from my life. Perhaps from Guatemala? Or Russia? All these places I've lived in, and carried a little taste back with me. Spain. England. Or even Maine. Where I began it all. My childhood.

Kat came and found me each time I left New Mexico. She began it all over again. And then she ended it, over and over. Ah, Kat. She forgot each time. She forgot that it was she who found me in all these far-off villages. Funny what I'm remembering.

I wonder what I'm forgetting, though.

I put the tea kettle on and start a fire. I listen to the kindling take and the whistle blow. Time for my mug of black coffee with honey. At the table, I pull out the notebook. I write out the people I'd like to talk to while I can. The ones I need to say more to. Always more. Kat, obviously! Maggie and Paula. David. Samantha, if I could talk to her. I still stay in touch with her brother, Tom. And Rian is in Spain still. And Mike and Charlie. Mike and I need to patch up some things between us soon. The last visit had ended in silence and anger. His, not mine, for once. Charlie and I never had anything come between us. I simply saw and accepted him, and I never told. Never told his secret.

As to my own family? I don't have one. Not blood family. All dead to me. Literally dead and buried, that is. And now? Just these friends who stuck with me over the years. The lovers, and the ones who truly knew how to love another, and who taught me as best they could. And that includes Eleanor, but she's been gone now almost three years. I miss her. Every day I miss her easy company.

I wish I could bring back all the friends now departed. Maybe I get to see them soon, but that's not really what I believe. It'd be a great bonus, though! And maybe I'd get to meet my birth parents again? I'm not sure how I feel about that. Would I recognize them? Weird thought.

I look at the list. Time to decide.

Who to call? Who to talk to? What do I say?

And how do I tell them? Without seeming pitiful or needy? I can't stand that side of this situation. Hmm. More coffee.

Maggie or Paula? Paula. She is one person I could talk to about anything, however crazy. And I always had.

Chapter Eleven

"Hey, there. Coffee ready?" I'd walked into the kitchen, feeling sleep wrecked again. My hair stuck out in all directions. Clothes were wrinkled and a tad smelly by now. I looked and felt rough. Not so great.

"Yeah, just about. Where did you get to last night?" Paula glanced up. "Guess."

"You don't seem happy about it, Joey."

"Nope. Not really." I held out a mug to fill. I sat at the table. The kids were out in the garden with Chris, helping him turn the compost.

Paula sat down next to me. "Well?"

"Messy. It got messy. Real fast. It was great to start with. I think. I'm not even sure about that. I just turned up. I watched the house for ages. Hours, I guess. I watched them make dinner. All lit up in the kitchen. Pasta and bread. I saw them talking and laughing and drinking red wine. And then I watched the girlfriend leave in the Land Rover, on her own. So then Kat was alone in the house. I was outside in the road, just sitting, wondering what to do. Wondering whether I'd go up and knock on the door or what. I smoked. I looked around. Nice set-up they have out there. You know that, though. Windy but really sweet. Well, I was daydreaming and suddenly woke up to Kat standing at my side. She was, well, I don't know. Pissed? Amused? Both? She told me to follow her inside.

"I got off the rock and followed her up the path, through the gardens and into the house. Big wooden doors, an open fireplace and nice old furniture everywhere. It felt like a family home. Not what I'd expected. Or hoped. It didn't feel like it was a home in the middle of any drama. No break-up energy, you know? So. She walked us into the kitchen and pulled out two glasses. 'Whiskey?' she said. I nodded and stood there. I didn't know what to say to her. Struck dumb like a teenager. It was horrible! She poured out two full shots and passed me one. 'Here's to stalkers!' she said and she drank it down in one gulp.

I started to stutter and explain, but she shut me off. She kissed me, deeply, almost knocking me down. I dropped my glass. I heard it shatter but she didn't stop. I burned up and pulled her in.

"'We have about an hour before Kelly comes back,' she said. And that was that. She threw me out of the house fifty minutes later. All undone, clothes untucked, ungrounded and yet completely ecstatic. We had hardly said a word to each other the whole time, the whole experience.

"Back outside, I stuttered again when I stood at the bike. I wanted to talk to her. But she cut me off. 'Not now, Joey,' she says. 'You have to leave now. Right now. Come back tomorrow night. At seven. I'll be alone. Now go.' And with that, she turned and walked inside. Nothing else. Didn't look back. Nothing. And now I'm damn confused."

After spewing all this out so quickly, I faded. I took a breath. I took a drink.

"Well, did you get your answer? Do you have a chance with her?"

I stood up and walked around the kitchen, picking up and putting down whatever was in reach. "Yes. No. Both. I fucking loved being with her. I loved fucking her. Oh, my God, the sex was incredible! Best I've ever had. No doubt about it. I felt so alive. We laughed tons, too. And it was like she wanted to get far inside me, not just the sex, but into who I am, why I am. And she held me close and made me see her, more than just her skin, beyond that. All of her. Fuck. Magical! I'm addicted. Want more."

"But?"

"There's more. Just as I was pulling onto the highway, Kat's ex drove up and stopped me. Kelly opened a window to talk to me, so I took off the helmet. I had no idea what to expect.

"'I guess you've been with my girlfriend.' That was the opener.

"'Kat?' I acted as innocent as possible while smelling of sex.

"'Kaitlin, yes.' Dark eyes stared at me, challenging me.

"'Yeah, I was there. Nice place. But from what I hear, you're not together any more. She tells me you two have broken up.' I smiled sweetly. I put my helmet back on and reached for my leather gloves.

"'She lied to you, then. You've been to my house. Does it look like she's moving out?' Her attitude shifted. 'And just so you're not surprised later on, let me tell you this—she likes her girls to be girls. And men, well, you won't be man enough for her. You haven't got a chance.' And with that, she drove off." I looked over at Paula and shrugged.

"So now what?"

"An affair, it'll have to be an affair, hidden from everyone they know. But I don't know that I can do that with her. Not like I haven't before. But this is magical. Different. I don't know what I can do. How to do this."

"Are you going back tonight?"

"I couldn't *not* go!" I sat back down. "Like I said, messy, eh? And it's all on her terms."

Chapter Twelve

I fire up the truck. I've decided to drive over the mountain to spend the morning with Paula. Chris died a few years ago. She's on her own, still in the place they built together so long ago. The kids? Maggie is nearby; maybe I'll look for her tomorrow. A visit per day? That sounds kinda nice to me.

The boys left town, with Charlie in California and Mikey, well, Mike now, he lives in Chicago with his girlfriend. He'll be back. It's about that time. Every few years, he comes back to say hello. He and I fought last time, though, not a pretty argument. I'd like to talk to him, clear the air between us. I miss him. We lived together at one point. I miss my young friend.

My truck is left over from the late '80s, a white Toyota four-by-four pick-up. The body is rusted out but the engine is solid. It helps that I left the country so often and it got to rest up, waiting for me from its space at Paula's place. As I get ready to leave for the day, I check on the water bowls for Fred and the cats. All looks good. I carry in a handful of kindling and set the fire for when I get home.

Might snow tonight. Each day is different. Remember that winter about two years ago? The snowstorm hit so hard and fast that we were all trapped for a week. Over three or four feet in one night. I'd been home. Had no idea. I woke, wanted to go outside to pee, and couldn't. The door was jammed with snow.

There I was, at sixty-nine or something, climbing out the kitchen window, slipping face first into the drifts. And getting deeper and deeper when I tried to get out and stand up, only to have Fred jump out and land on top of me. I laughed so hard that I peed myself! If anyone had seen me, I'd never have heard the end of it. Lucky I live alone. If Eleanor had still been around, I can imagine her falling over laughing with me.

I'm about to get in the truck when it occurs to me: What am I thinking? It's too early to go visiting. Not that Paula will be sleeping, but it just feels too early. Seven o'clock, maybe? Did I eat yet? I don't think so. I had some coffee. That part I remember. So I turn off the engine. At least I know it works still! It's been a week since I last drove anywhere. I'm not driving much these days.

Well, now. Food? Or a walk? Or both? Yeah, both.

I put the sausages on to cook slowly, and then whistle for my pets. Yep, all of them like to walk with me. The boy cat leads the way, up the path and across the ridge. It used to be Fred up front, but he's at my pace these days. The girl cat comes along, too but, to be honest, I think she'd like me to carry her on my shoulders. Such a princess, eh?

It's chilly but not bad. I look out west and see the beginning wisps of snow clouds. I can't smell them yet. Did you know you could smell snow coming? It's subtle, but there is a definite hint in the air, in the nostrils. Takes practice, that's all, practice to slow down and notice.

I follow Kit-Kit and we amble through the piñon and the junipers, past some cholla cactus. The grass shivers in silvery waves as the wind begins to pick up. I believe snow is truly on its way. The golden sky lights up the mountains behind.

Funny how I ended up on what I consider Paula's mountains. The south side of the Ortiz, that's where you'll find my land. Forty acres of untouched ridge top. I look out west and northwest. Huge open mesas and valleys fill the landscape, until the Jemez Mountains block the horizon beyond. A flat mesa divides the land and drops off suddenly, leading into the pueblos at the Rio Grande. It's a glorious place to live, and I am blessed to have my own little home within it. No wonder I kept coming back. How many years now? How many times did I leave?

Well, there was that first time I met Kat. You see, I've lived here in spurts, short bursts of settling. Short meaning four or five years at a time. Build a home, settle in, try to love someone, first Kat, and then anyone that wasn't Kat, and then? Then I'd leave again. I'd just leave again.

Let's see, where to? Well, all over the place. Europe mostly, Europe and the Americas. And then I'd come back again. Paula and family take me in. I start all over again. Bump into Kat and, well, you get the idea. Off I go. Went. Now, though, I stay. This is home. Kat be damned.

I wonder what I have in the trunk for David. I'd love to find a tool or knife from far away. Like Russia. Yeah, do I still have that silver pocket watch from Moscow? Or was it Leningrad? I'll need to make sure I have the right story! A keepsake. A reminder. A souvenir. That's French for remembering, an object with memories. Well, I think that's it. I can look it up at the house. Tons of books.

Oh, the books, what do I do with all of them? I can't take them with me, can I? Who might like them? Charlie, he is the most home proud, and he has a sense of culture and literature in common with me. We used to sit on the porch, read and talk about anything and everything. Good kid he was.

Fred is slowing down. It's his hips. Mine are fine. I'm still pretty sprightly. No sign of impending doom. A few headaches, but that is manageable. We stop at the overlook. Throughout my time here, I've pulled a few flat rocks together and made a seat for myself, with part shade and full vistas. Can't be beat.

I crave a smoke, but I gave them up years ago. Maybe ten years? Or was it more? Who cares, though? It's not going to kill me. I want to roll a smoke for old times' sake. Maybe David has some. Or I can just buy some in

Madrid. It's no ghost town these days. Fascinating village. Thriving mining town till the '50s, but was closed in 1959 and the company left it. Empty.

Tried to sell it. No buyers. Then, one by one, the hippies and the artists came. Unafraid to take on the derelict wooden houses, and slowly the homes were all lived in. Maybe three or four hundred people now. I know many of them, neighbors of mine, in a sense. The store. The tavern. The coffee shop. Us old-timers hang around and talk for hours on end at Java café—another local institution. Some thirty years in business. Not bad, eh? And many of the homes are now galleries and crafts stores for the tourists who think we're a freak show here for their benefit. Joke's on them, the prices we charge. That's a whole other story. Mine demands breakfast. Time to walk back.

I stand and bow to the world around me. "Thank you. Much appreciated." And I turn down the path, making my way home.

It doesn't matter what changes in the big world, my life seems to stay pretty much the same. I make stuff at home. I grow food. I cut wood and haul water. I had a lover once who fell for me because I lived the monk's lifestyle. In her eyes, that's what this was. Nothing extra. A few changes of clothes. A rustic home with all I needed. Animals. Warmth.

Sweet homes I've had. Yeah. For so many decades, it's been the same. A sustainable life. Laziness, to be truthful, is the main reason. I'd prefer more time at home even if that means less work, therefore less money. Time has always been more precious to me than the money in my pocket. I suppose that's why I ended up as a freelance writer, doing whatever was needed as and when it came up. Those were the years I got paid to write about the alternative and 'cool' lifestyles.

One time I stayed on a commune in the South. They lived off-grid, grew food, raised animals, made honey and lived independent of mainstream society. That was in the '80s. I felt so at ease. I didn't expect to, well, with it being Tennessee and so conservative in many ways. Didn't think they'd like someone like me. But they gave me such a warm welcome. Maybe they just didn't look too closely? Anyway, I'd needed to be there that winter, oh yeah, I'd needed a warm welcome. To feel at home with other people. My heart was aching yet again.

I'd driven away from Santa Fe, all desperate to start over. I'd had the commission to find and write about intentional communities across the country. I used that as a reason to leave my home. To leave after another intense episode with Kat.

By that time, I was in my mid-thirties. Not much older. We'd been to-gether a few years; finally, we had come together. No more affairs. And I'd built a home for us. Near Taos in Northern New Mexico. Built it myself. Made the adobe bricks. Hauled the twenty-six foot vigas for the roof. It was incredible. We had a studio space for her wood shop and sculptures, with huge south-facing windows. I had a room where I could write. The bedroom for us was a loft platform, up high within the fourteen-foot high ceilings, looking out over the cliffs. I plastered the straw-bales with local adobe clay and I poured a beautiful red mud floor. She adored it. I was so unbelievably happy. For us.

And soon after I finished, she told me that she wanted to be with Mark, her ex-husband. Not with me.

I'd spent the last few years creating this home for us to share, for our friends to enjoy with us, and for us to create and play in. But no. That wasn't her plan. It was no longer convenient to have me around. I'd done my job, hadn't I? I hadn't seen this coming. I had no idea she had other ideas for the home or for herself.

I was crushed. I crashed. And I waited for her to come back to me. Emotionally. Instead, she raged at me for staying. She wanted me to leave.

To walk away. Like I had done before. I was determined to stay. Not to run away. Not even to walk away, looking back with each step of mine.

I stayed. And she hated me for it.

Chapter Thirteen

One day, she cornered me in the living room and told me she'd made a date with her ex later that week. We had a bad day. Silent treatment. I didn't know what was going on. Why she'd do this to us. It had taken so long for us to get together as a couple. What the hell was going on?

I didn't get it. So I started smoking real early. I had a few beers, too. I ignored her. She spat insults at me on and off the whole day. I worked in my studio. She painted. And then started screaming at me from her room. "You are just like your mother!"

"What the fuck do you mean by that? You never met her." I came to the doorway and stared. Confused. Hurt.

Kat laughed in my face. "You told me. I know her through you. This drinking of yours instead of. Well, let's put it this way. No wonder your dad killed her."

"What?"

She spewed out all this shit. Taking the crappiest times of my stories, of being a kid in Maine, on the small island that was home until I turned eight. My fucked-up family. Kat, the one who knew me so deeply, said all this crap. About me. About my mom. And then about why she hated my being here. And then she sobbed and whispered, "I hate you for making me love you. I wish you'd just leave me alone."

"What the fuck, Kat? What the fuck are you saying?"

"I want you to leave. Go."

"But this is my home. Our home. I built this for us."

"It's my land."

"But I made this for us. Kat?"

" I told you, it's over. I can't live with you."

49

"Why not? You love me."

Silence and tears.

"You loved me once. How many years have we been doing this? Get used to it. I'm here. I'm sticking around this time. You love me. Right?"

"Joey. Stop. Right now. Stop. It's all in your head." She stood between the front door and me. I wanted to leave. But I didn't. She started screaming at me to leave, but wouldn't let me. Telling me how it's all my fault. She'd bought the land. Not for us. But for her. That I'd invited myself. She didn't know how to stop me. She was scared of me. The last two years, she knew. Knew she wanted to get back with Mark. He was easy on her. And I'm too much. Too intense. Too different. For her. Not enough. For her.

She hit me, over and over, hitting me on the chest; pushing me away and then pulling me back to punch me again. Holding me against her before crying and hitting me again.

"What the fuck's going on?" I screamed back. "You asked me to come here. To build a home here."

"I didn't!"

"Yes, you did!"

"I did not!"

I almost laughed. And then she did.

I stepped away, out of reach. I looked at her, stunned at what we'd come to. I stood next to the steps to the loft. "Come here."

Kat frowned and then offered me a wicked knowing smile. "Your rules or mine?"

"Mine. Come here."

And she did.

You see, it wasn't always on her terms.

A week later, I'd left for Tennessee. I'd had that writing assignment. It was good timing for us to take a break. She still wanted me gone. I still loved her too much. Too much for the both of us.

I'd driven the truck across I-40 and took the road south when I hit Tennessee. It was November and cold. I drove and drove even though it was dark and the directions seemed complicated. Tired as I was, I wanted to get there for the night. It had taken three days to cross from Santa Fe. I finally found the dirt road to take me toward the land. The Farm. Strangely enough, Kat had told me only a few months before about a dream of hers, her staying at this place I'd never heard of at that point. A commune in the backwoods of a conservative Baptist county. Why she would think of this, I don't know. Why I ended up there only months later, it's one of those cosmic jokes, if you ask me.

Anyway, the road was a single track hugging the side of a tobacco field. I drove carefully. After three miles, I saw the turn to the right and drove down there. I parked where everyone else did. I walked down to the house. I had no idea what to expect.

I'd found a huge wooden cabin full of warmth and honest-to-goodness friendliness.

"You're Joey, right? We heard about you from John. You met him in LA a while ago. He's here, well, at his place but he'll be here for dinner in half an hour or so. So, yeah, he told us you wanted to write about us for some magazine. Cool!" This was Jane. I found every one created new names for themselves when they got here. New beginnings.

"What do you want us to call you? Think about it!"

"How long you staying? You can stay in my room if you like!"

Five or six men and women surrounded me, teased me and invited me to join them.

"Who do you want to stay with? Your pick!"

I grinned and asked to not have to choose right now. "Tired, you know?"

They all laughed and then one of them sat me down on the sofa next to the woodstove.

"Maybe tomorrow I can show you around. The bathhouse. The gardens. The individual cabins scattered on the land. I'll tell you the history and the intentions of the place. And no expectations, okay? I have a boyfriend. I don't want another lover!"

Jane introduced me to her sweetheart, Billy, and then we all sat and chatted before dinner.

"You look like you have a broken heart." Billy spoke quietly.

I didn't know how to answer him. But then I told him of the lovers' fight, Kat claiming the home I'd built, her wanting her ex, and that I needed a break. To write and re-think a few things.

"You're welcome to stay a while 'til you know what you want to do."

"Thanks, Billy. I need to rest up. Decide what we do next. With the home, with us. If there is an 'us.' I don't know."

"Well, I know that dinner is going to be good! I helped make it. Potatoes and chiles from the garden. Homemade wine. A little something to smoke, and cookies from the solar oven. How's that for a broken heart?" He grinned and stood up. "Let's eat."

I stayed three months. Hadn't planned to, but I did. I took on the name Danny. I wrote. I soaked in the wood-heated hot tub. Jane and I hiked in the hills surrounding the Farm. I read and read. I made fires. I taught Billy how work with wood, to make furniture.

They taught me how to harvest water and grow food for a community of twenty. We all cooked and cleaned and built together. Easy. Easy on me.

Just the tonic I needed before I headed back in March. I needed to finish with Kat, once and for all, finish this affair of ours. This relationship.

Chapter Fourteen

Breakfast consists of sausages and eggs and tortillas. Perfect. My mind wanders as I cook. The animals rest out on the steps. I watch clouds forming over near the Jemez Mountains. The air is getting chillier as I eat. I'm excited to go over to see Paula, but first I'd like to look in the trunk and find the perfect gift for her grandson. For David. I'm thinking of the Russian pocket watch. Once I'm done eating, I'll go back inside and see what I have. See if I can find it. See if I can remember when I picked it up.

Huh, that's right. I'd just turned forty-nine the year of Glasnost. Of Gorbachev. Suddenly, Russia was so much easier to visit. And so I did. I'd been living for a few months in Southern Germany at the time. I'd started working on a new book while in Freiberg-in-Breisgau, popping over to Strasburg in France for the incredible food, going to research other intentional communities near both Rome and Madrid and then, on weekends, I went driving to Zurich for the parties with some new friends. For six months, that was my daily experience, a mix of great beer, fine food and lots of new places and people. A hard life!

So anyway, I signed up on some tourist trip to Moscow and Leningrad, as it was still known at that point. A hotel in each city provided a tour guide to take the tourists around. The Moscow Circus. The Ballet. All very cultural. I loved the idea of treating myself. I hadn't been on that kind of a vacation ever. Like I said. A treat.

At the huge Moscow hotel, I walked up to my room. I'd spent the day in museums and wanted to sleep for an hour or so. I was looking forward to a nap. A Babushka sat at the end of each floor by the elevators, keeping hold of the keys. I had to give the one on my floor my passport in order to get my key.

She gave me an odd look. Said something and pointed to my room, but wouldn't give me a key. I had no idea what was going on. I carried my daypack down the corridor. My room was open. Maybe she'd said they were cleaning it or something? I knocked and stepped inside.

Kat was sprawled in the chair next to the window overlooking the city. She had a bottle of whiskey and two plastic cups with ice.

"What are you doing here?"

"Want one?"

"Well, yes, but Kat! What the fuck are you doing here? How'd ya find me? Why did they let you in?"

Kat came and held out her hand for me. I reached for her instinctively. No thought. She pulled me inside and closed the door behind us, away from prying old ladies paid to spy on us. She took the bag off my shoulder and removed my thick black jacket and the hat.

"Hey, I want a hat like this. Did you get it here? Looks real." She looked in the earflaps and found the Russian words. She looked at me. "Can we get me one, too? I'd look great in one of these!"

It was local; she was right. An old one, though. One my dad gave me when I was a kid. From his army days or something. Beautifully made, black fur on the outside with silk inside. Warm beyond belief.

Kat offered me a drink.

"Kat?"

"Yes, sweetheart?"

"Why are you here?"

"I told them I'm your wife."

"And they let you in, just like that?"

"Admittedly, they're a bit confused! But, I carried on as if nothing was unusual about us being together. The Babushka held onto my passport. Anyway, I told them it's your fiftieth birthday this weekend."

"I'm forty-nine."

"I know, Joey. And you turn fifty on Sunday."

She handed me the whiskey. I sank it. "No. I turn forty-nine on Sunday. I'm forty-eight."

"You're not. You're forty-nine. About to be fifty."

"I am not."

"You are, too!" She looked again. "Are you sure? Turning fifty is a big deal."

"Next year, then, is the big deal."

"Oh. Surprise, anyway!" She pulled out a crappy pink paper hat and a red candle from her pocket and held them out to me. "Happy almost-fiftieth birthday, Joey!"

How could I not laugh?

"The hotel thinks it's your birthday. The big one. So expect something from them. The tour guide likes you, too. A little too much for my liking. But anyway. Maybe we can all go out to dance and have a few vodkas out in the city? I'd love that. And don't forget, I need a new hat!"

The next morning, we woke early and headed out the door. The Babushka took our key and noted down the time in her book. Six a.m.

Kat giggled as we stood waiting for the elevator to take us downstairs. "Do you think someone will follow us?"

"I have no idea! Maybe. You might get us in trouble again. Remember the train trip through Spain? Getting us thrown off in that little town? And then sitting on the station's steps when Rian cycled past us? Talk about coincidence. I never even knew that she'd moved back there. Wasn't it great that we got to stay with her for a few days?"

"And your point is? To make me jealous again?"

"You were jealous? Really? You never told me that."

56

Kat slapped me playfully across the head just as we walked out the front doors of the hotel. In front of us stood some five or six taxis, at least it seemed that way. The driveway swung down to the right, and toward the main street into Moscow. The temperature had dropped again. Last night, it had been ten degrees. And at dawn, we felt every one of them. Kat hung on tight to me. My body warmth. Or a leftover sweetness from a night spent deeply inside each other. I didn't ask which. It was always best not to ask.

We followed the paved road toward the river, now fully frozen. February is the coldest time to visit Russia, but I'd loved the stories set in the deep country winters of Moscow and beyond. John Le Carre and those thrillers and cold war mysteries. I had to come at this time of year. Kat is much more the warm weather woman. Most happy when scantily dressed and tanned, yet she always has black and red cowboy boots on, whatever the temperature outside.

She didn't complain. Too excited by our naughty disappearance from the tour guide's watchful eyes. We were looking to buy her a hat. Black market dealings. I knew enough for us to find the right bench to wait at. Sure enough, along came a six-foot beefy man all wrapped up in many layers. I nodded. He sat.

Kat watched me and smiled to herself. Holding my hand on her lap, she and I talked to the unnamed man. He opened his huge coat to show us two hats like mine. Newer than mine, but close enough.

Kat clamped tight onto my hand. I took one and passed it to her. She tried it on. Too big— I had to laugh when it fell to her nose. The next hat was shabbier but when she put it on, Kat laughed out loud in delight. Yes. That was the one for her. We haggled over the price for a minute, but half-heartedly. I never meant to pay less than whatever he wanted. Whatever she wanted. It was that important to me. Kat and I shook his hand, thanked him and walked off.

"Wait a minute, Joey. I need to ask him something."

"You do? Okay, let's walk back."

"No. You stay here and watch out for a minute. I'll be back."

She ran off under the bridge. I heard her call out to him, then the voices and some laughter. Hers. His. Then she skipped back up the steps to me. Smiling to herself but refusing to say why.

My birthday itself came with tea from the Babushka and a candle from the guide, who hadn't been happy with us after our morning out alone. Oh, well. The tea was incredibly strong. We couldn't stop talking afterwards. Luckily we had a few hours to ourselves before the night's excursion to the nightclub on the top floor of the hotel.

"Live Russian Band," the guide told us proudly. "Many tourists love to dance to Live Russian Band."

It was to be a birthday night out with the other tourists on the trip with us. A gang of ten Americans and Brits. Drinking up a storm. Yep.

But first, Kat ran me a bath. She sat on the edge of it, wearing nothing but her slip, the hat and her boots. A fine figure of a woman. You'd never guess she was in her late forties with those defined muscles and a clearly fit, healthy body. I could never get enough of her, and even staring was pretty satisfying. Well, after a few hours together in bed, it could be enough.

She told me, "William wants a divorce.'

I lay in the hot water under her gaze. I said nothing. What could I say? I had heard this often in the course of our affair. Break-ups always prompted her to come look for me wherever I was. She always did find me. I never wondered how. I put it down to Maggie.

Anyway, I said nothing. I waited. It all came out. What did get me was her honesty with William.

"He knew. About us. He always had known. I told him that first week-end I spent at his house. He liked the idea. Fantasized about a three-some. I set him straight on that one, though. 'Joey's mine. And I don't share.' Will took it in his stride. But something shifted for us, for him. Last week. When I told him I had to come find you for your fiftieth birthday."

"Forty-ninth." I corrected her.

"Well, when I told him I had to find you, he threw a fit. Screaming at me to leave, to leave him alone. That if I needed you, I should be with you and not him. I tried to explain. I told him everything."

"Which is what, these days? What is 'everything?' I don't know."

Kat stopped. Surprised. "Well, I love you. I always have."

"But?" I asked.

"How about an 'and,' instead? *And* you drive me crazy after a few months. A few weeks, sometimes."

"True enough. Anyway, what happened with William then?"

"Not good. Jealous of you. Hates me for not being satisfied with him alone. Same old story, right? When will I meet someone who lets me love who I love?"

I couldn't answer that. Too close to our own problems.

I stood up to get out of the bath and Kat passed me a towel. Not a soft one like you'd find at the Hilton, this was more of a '70s leftover that barely covered your ass. That visual brought Kat back to being her charming self. She pointed and laughed hard. I slapped her with my towel and chased her into the bedroom with the two single beds. She jumped one. I followed, dropping the towel in my rush to catch her. We fell over the second bed and landed in a heap next to the window.

"Hey, Joey, look at that city out there. Isn't it weirdly wonderful? I loved walking through the government stores this afternoon. So strange, though. Empty. All very empty and gray. Oh! I have something for you!"

She stood up and helped me onto the bed next to her. "Here you are, Joey." She handed me a sock of mine with something hidden in the toes. "Sorry, I couldn't find any wrapping paper!"

I upended the sock into my palm. A silver pocket watch fell out. A detailed picture of the Kremlin had been etched into it. It was well worn and had obviously been much loved. I listened to the ticking as I opened and closed it. "Oh, Kat. Thank you. It's beautiful."

"I do love you, Joey."

Chapter Fifteen

"Didn't you two have another one of your huge fights that night?" Paula asks with her usual tact.

"No. That was later, in Leningrad. At a different hotel. A different nightclub. Yeah. We'd had such a great week together. A honeymoon is how it felt. Most of the time! Anyway, it wasn't so much us fighting that was the problem. It's because I hit that local fella. That's why we got kicked out. He didn't like having vodka thrown in this face. And I didn't like him pushing Kat around. You remember, right? Big old mess when we left Russia. But it got Kat to see my apartment in Germany before I came back here. But. The watch. What do you think? Can I give this to David?"

Paula takes the watch from me and studies it again. She holds it up to her ears. She smells it. She feels its weight. "Yes, you know he'd love it. Anything from you is gold to him. But why? And what would Kat say if she knew? You've had it, what, thirty years? Why give it away now?"

I take a deep breath. "I have cancer."

"Oh." Paula sits back in her armchair and stares at me. Neither of us speaks for ten minutes or so. She watches the chickens in the yard. I watch her. She turns to me finally. "How bad?"

"Pretty bad. I can't afford to do anything. I want to just let it be. Stay home. Be at home."

"I'm so sorry, Joey. I don't know what to say."

I stand. I look around. I smile. "Got a smoke? Sure would be nice right now! So much for quitting."

Paula points me to the tin on the table beside me. "Tobacco and pot. Whichever you want. It's right there."

I open the box and help myself. The thing about old friends, not old in years per se but those people who know you so well, I don't have to talk. She knows me. She knows how scared for my animals I am, for my home. Her first question, though, is, "Have you told Kat?"

"No." I'm quiet. Then I say, "You're the first. Well. Dr. Nan is helping me however she can. I don't know how to say it. How to tell anyone. You're the first. How did I do?"

Paula smiles weakly. "Okay, I guess. I wish I'd known earlier so I could have been with you for all of this."

"Not much has happened. I won't let the doctors poke me more than necessary. I don't want to prolong this. Just be ready for it, that's all I can do. Are you okay, my sweet friend?"

"No. Not really. Sad. Incredibly sad. Wish I could do something to make it go away. There's nothing to be done? Are you sure?"

I shrug. "There is, but I don't want to do it. I've had such a full life. Why keep at it? Why put us all through more drama and pain? I kinda want to just fade away. Say goodbye and go. Wouldn't you?"

Paula shrugs this time. Sad, like she said. "I don't know. Can we go for a walk together? Now? I need time to, well, I need time."

I think about making a joke about time and me not being best friends but I hold it in. I stand up and hold my hand out to her. She reaches for me. We head down the driveway and up the arroyo toward the old goldmines. Familiar turf for the both of us. Cholla cactus. Russian olive trees. Junipers. Piñon. Tuft grasses. Sand. Rocks. Rabbits. Ravens. Mice and rats.

"Do you want me to tell anyone for you, Joey?"

"No, that's not your job. I need to do that. But I wanted to tell you first. I'd like to talk to Maggie. David. You three are my closest family these days."

"And Kat?"

"She is still my beloved."

I walk some more before I admit that I'm terrified of telling her. "I don't know why, but I am so scared to talking to her right now. Each time a truck pulls up, I want to hide in case it's her. I ignore the phone, too."

"Nothing new there! You always have!" Paula is coming back to herself. Joking is the best response I could ask for. Pity is the worst. She holds my hand again. Sentimentality is my weakness. I try not to cry.

Paula tells me, "I love you, my friend. You are the best friend I ever had. And I'm so, so, very glad."

I tear up and keep walking. After a few moments, I whisper, "Thank you Paula. For everything."

She squeezes my hand and says nothing. We don't need to say it out loud.

The mountains have the pink glow of a storm. The breeze is picking up and I see the clouds moving in. Paula and I walk up the hillside until we stop at the fence line. She looks back down into the valley between here and Santa Fe. I see the snow on the Sangre de Cristos over forty miles away. To the right, the west that is, there is emptiness, pure unadulterated mesa New Mexican ranch land. It's so beautiful.

And I have Paula to thank for bringing me here, for keeping me here. Over and over she gave me a safe home to recuperate within its peace and acceptance. The worst and the happiest times of my life came from this desert's tranquility and her family's welcome. How blessed am I to have a friend like Paula? More than I can ever express.

"Remember when I asked if I could stay a while?"

"Of course! One month turned into three into six, and then it was almost a year later that you finally left us!"

"You make it sound like you didn't want me!"

"You know better than that! You lived in the little cabin that winter. Lived in it for the rest of the year. I still love sitting in there. Makes me think of when the kids were so little. No wonder Maggie and the boys love you so much. You spent all that time reading to them, out on the porch or in front of the fire in the afternoons."

"Purely selfless reasons. I wanted you and Chris to get to mess around and make me some more kids to play with. Always was easier around the youngsters. It's you women that confused me."

Paula laughs. "You liar! It was only ever Kat that confused you. Hell, she confused me, too. And I just witnessed the messiness through you. I never had such a dramatic love affair. Chris and me, it was always just good friends and fun sex. Family and home were the focus. Not the high adventure and fighting you two got into."

We walk some more and we find a great tree to sit against. Paula asks if I want to tell her any details about the cancer.

"No, no details. Not yet. But I will tell you. I promise."

Paula sits quietly next to me, and then leans against my shoulder. I like the touch of her warmth. Human connection, my driving force. That's been my only reason to stay around. To stay alive.

I stroke her hair and start to reminisce out loud with her about those first years in New Mexico. The studio we built for her family. My finding afternoons and nights with Kat whenever I could. The trip she and I took up into the Jemez Mountains together, and her teaching me to drive up there on the gravel roads. Working with Chris and enjoying his green thumb. Teaching Maggie to read. Settling into a family life, even if it wasn't really mine. I'd liked it. Enough to keep coming back.

We drift off, silent for what seems like hours. The sun keeps us warm enough to lose track.

"You daydreaming again, Joey?"

"Funny, David keeps asking me that. Yeah, my mind is all over the place these days. I suppose I'm trying to make sense of everything."

"Well, if you come up with any answers, let me know. Life is kind of a mystery, if you ask me."

"Really? But Paula, yours has been so easy and straightforward. No offense, that's what I kept trying to make happen with Kat and, well, the others, too. But…"

Paula looks up, surprised. "You think we had it easy? Don't be so patronizing! Chris struggled for so long, and it was so hard for me to watch both of you. Not so easy to raise the kids and the two of you, especially you, Joey. You came and went. Up and down. I never knew when to welcome you back. Or when to send you away. Kind of like you told Kat once: It was on your terms."

I'm quiet. I hadn't thought what it might be like for her. My breakdowns. The hospital stuff. Kat showing up and then the stormy emotional aftermath.

"Did it bug you? My leaving all the time?"

"Yes. No. I don't know. It was hard, that's all. I had to say something if you were going to think it wasn't hard for me. I love you. But damn, you put us through a lot."

I start to tear up. She doesn't notice, I'm glad to say. "I'm sorry, Paula."

"Oh, Joey. That's not why I'm saying this. It's nothing new. Haven't we talked about this before? How the drama drained you? And, well, Kat, too, she's as much the cause for all the ups and downs. Not easy for someone like you. For anyone, really."

"Did you like her? Do you now?"

Paula takes a breath, a deep one and then explains that she understood the need we had for each other, or rather she saw it, but doesn't get it, not really. Paula loves in such a gentle and open manner that the extremes of my passion for Kat is beyond her experience. I'm not sure I would wish it on anyone.

Paula stands up. "Let's walk back. I'm getting cold. Did you hear the storm is coming in tonight? Maybe mid-afternoon?"

I nod my head, and say how David had dropped off more wood for me last night. "I'll be fine," I tell her.

"And when you get sick? Sicker? What do we do?"

"I don't know. I haven't thought it through yet. Let's walk home. Make some of your tea. Do you have any cookies for me?"

"Food. Food. Food. Typical distraction tactics, Joey. But, yes, walk, tea and then we talk. Okay?"

We walk in silence, both upset. Not much to say right now. The mountains become a hazy soft blue behind us as we head down the hill. I close the jacket up and pull out my woolen cap. Still got it. Pretty good, huh?

Once inside, I make us a fire, and Paula sorts out some snacks and peppermint tea. At the table in the kitchen, we both sit and face each other. Now what? Who starts?

Paula does. "So, when you get sick, how do we help you? What will you need? Do you even know?"

I shrug reluctantly. "Dr. Nan keeps trying to talk to me about this, but I haven't let her yet. I needed some time. I think I wanted to talk to you first, too. See where you want to fit in to this. I have my savings so I can buy my supplies for the time being. Not enough for medical help, not really. Dr. Nan knew Mary at the clinic. It's out of love for her that she's doing this for free. More of a friend by now."

"I'm not surprised. You have that effect on people. What does she say, exactly?"

"To call my family, my closest friends and invite them for Thanksgiving, that it's time to say goodbye."

"Oh, my God, Joey! That bad? Ohshitohshitohshit." Paula is stunned. "That's too soon, Joey. I want more time. Much more time with you."

"I do, too. But there isn't any more. I've had my allotted time for this round. Not much I can do about it. Except be thankful for what I've had."

Paula is crying.

"Like being here with your family, and making a home for myself. Like the years with Samantha in Guatemala, back in the '70s. Working in Spain after that. All the lovers, and the loving, and even the heartbreaks. Eleanor and being with her in Britain and building a home with her here. And watching your kids grow up. Your grandson, too."

"Maybe the Thanksgiving is a good idea," she offers.

I smile weakly. "It's growing on me, too. Maybe, huh? A gathering of the clan, the tribe."

"Will you invite Kat?"

"No. I can't. I can't do that to us again. A final goodbye with her? I just can't," and I start sobbing. My head hits the table and I cry.

I can't. I just can't.

Chapter Sixteen

The brightly colored school bus took the chickens and me through the open-air market in Antigua. The town opened up in front of us within the chaos of a Saturday night. Streets were packed with vendors carrying their wares balanced on heads; others sat and sold snacks on the corners and the steps to the old churches. Cobblestones and gravel roads took us through the alleys and lanes and I was amazed at how this bus could squeeze round tight turns. The pastel colored adobe homes lined the narrow paths up and out of town and into the next villages in the mountains.

I sat, packed in with all the locals, shivering in the late spring's dark night. I held my small green backpack on my knees. Music blared over the loud speaker. Military gatekeepers watched the bus drive by, holding the guns loosely at their sides. I kept my head low and hid behind the cap. I avoided staring at the police. There I was, a gringo with a bunch of Mayans. Odd one out.

Guatemala was a political mess, fighting in the mountains. Ladinos held on tightly to their governmental power, and kicked out at any threats. Fighting took place all over the country, no longer just in the urban centers. Insurgents hid in the hills and the American- backed army fought them when and where they could. And the peasants, the indigenous peoples, they were trying to live the way they knew best. Both sides of the story were full of rage and pain. Murder of the Mayans became a national sport for some. And the Mayans hid in the mountains, up far away along hidden tracks, through the thick woods. Guerrilla and military taking it out on each other in the villages. Killing each other in the name of peace. In the name of justice or vengeance. I didn't know the difference.

I was on my way to the Highlands, to Panajachel. To help, however I could. I had a green thumb. I could help grow food. I knew about making cheap and easy homes with local materials, and I knew about reusing water from the roofs and streams for the gardens. I thought I could teach them. How fucking arrogant of me.

And I was terrified. I was not supposed to be here. Not safe for Americans. For tourists. I thought I was different, though. Again, how fucking arrogant of me.

I knew Samantha and her brother, Tom, from a brief visit to California. They now lived in Panajachel, working with the locals, building a school and helping teach kids to read. Samantha had asked me to come down, challenging me to explore the world since I'd never left the U.S. before. She thought that I ought to do it before I turned thirty. Travel, volunteer and learn. And now I could. I had the funds to take off; after another good harvest with Chris and Paula had given me money in my pocket.

I'd taken the buses through Mexico, days on end, curled up in the small kid-sized seats, eating tamales and bananas, and slowly picking up the language. I had an ear for it. Learned fast. But now I was so tired, drained by all the sounds and the tension around me. I wanted to relax, but that I couldn't do until I found Sam and Tom.

Hours later, the bus pulled into Pana, and the driver called out for the gringo to get out here. He asked who I knew, so I described Tom and then his younger sister, Samantha.

He smiled. "Muy Guapa, que no? Esta por alla, a la derecha. Buen suerte!"

I stepped out and walked to the right as told, and yes, there she was. Sitting on the steps to this beat-up home, the plaster falling off, the shutters hanging lopsided. I watched as she chatted to these three local girls, dressed in the traditional skirts and blouses. I noticed the dirty bare feet poking out underneath. Samantha was chatting away and they had a book between them, passed from one hand to another, the kids excitedly talking and laughing. Sam glowed. Her naturally pale skin had turned golden with the outdoor life, her long light-brown hair tied back and she wore a loose dress over her slender body. She looked up and noticed me.

"Joey! How great to see you! I can't believe it—you're here." She stood quickly and the kids stepped back. She said something to them and the girls giggled. One of them came up to me and held her hand out to shake.

"My name is Maria. I'm ten. How old are you?"

I laughed out loud. "Very old!"

Sam came over and hugged me and then kissed me, claiming me as her lover. Simple as that.

"Mi novio," she explained to the giggling girls. They ran off squealing in disgust and delight.

"What did that mean?"

Sam smiled, and told that it should be pretty obvious after her kiss.

"Oh!" I put my backpack down and hugged tightly. "Thanks for such a warm welcome."

She took me inside the two-room house and closed the door behind us. She kissed me deeply and I forgot how tired I was, how hungry. I needed this more than anything else right now.

We took our time and held each other and I explored the taste and feel of her against me. I had not been with anyone for months and I'd felt every day without touch, the absence shutting me down, but now she was reclaiming my senses. I was waking up after the slumber of aloneness. I stepped back and we started chatting about Pana, living here, and her home. Easy, this felt easy and natural and so comfortable.

The wooden table next to a gas ring burner was her kitchen. Three chairs, oddly matching with bright paint. A bucket of water stood in the corner. Through the one other door I saw her bed, a mattress on the floor with two woolen blankets of the most intricate weaving and designs. Blues and greens swirled across each other in an echo of the landscape I'd seen for the last few days.

"Made by Josefa next door. Isn't it beautiful? Every night I go to sleep wrapped in her loving hands."

She poured me a glass of water and sat me down at the table. "It's good to see you, Joey. I didn't know if you'd make it on your own!"

"I wasn't sure for a few times there. My Spanish is coming along, though. I have a little dictionary with me so that helped. I'm glad I did it. Just left. I was talking to a bunch of folks before I left and everyone's freaked out by what's going on here. Is it pretty bad?"

She nodded her head. "I can't even describe it to you. I have to keep myself low-key. There's the army everywhere. People disappearing every so often. I get scared at times, especially when Tom heads into the smaller village for a week at a time. But the neighbors around here take care of me, warn me when to keep a low profile. I make it look like I'm here to write a novel, no threat to anyone."

"But that's not all, right?"

"No, I help in the school, and I'm teaching the girls some English for the tourists who sometimes come stay on the lake. So they can make more money from them. Oh, you probably didn't even see it yet, huh? Too dark. That'll be a treat in the morning. I'll walk down there with you."

She told me more about the people she'd met in the last three months being there. She talked about Tom's trips and how he wouldn't tell her where he went or why. "To protect me if the police came looking."

I started to fade fast, my eyes closing as she talked and warmed up some beans for me. I ate slowly, too tired to answer questions but for one.

"Do you want to stay with me as my lover or as my friend?" she asked.

"Lover."

She took me to bed.

In the morning, we walked down to the waterfront. It was incredible. A lake some five miles wide lay surrounded by three volcanoes. Sam explained that for the Mayan culture, this was where the world began. There were ten or more villages scattered long the edges, the only place to settle as the volcanoes and mountains simply dropped into the clear blue water. There was nothing soft or gentle about these hills. Dramatic, dark, thick jungles covered them, untouched and unclaimed. Apparently you could walk to a few small towns from this side of Lake Atitlan, or you took the boats. The 'Lanchas" were the local bus system, with the men rowing you across from one corner to another, with your market goods, chickens, cloth, or whatever you wanted and needed to transport. Pana was the main market town nearby. The boats were small, wooden and solidly made. I couldn't fathom rowing across the water.

"The afternoons are the worst time. The winds pick up at three or four and rage for hours after that. Waves have tossed people overboard a few times since I've been here. Tom goes out in the boats anytime he's asked."

"What's he doing here?"

"I'll tell you later when we get home. Come with me, there's a place for some strong coffee. You still like coffee in the mornings?"

"Yeah," I grinned, "can't help it. I'm hungry, too. Can we get something to eat?"

"You'd better get used to eating less. Not much food around here for anyone. Look and you'll see no one has an extra ounce of weight on them."

"But I brought a bunch of money. I can buy us something."

"Yes, you could. We could live like kings here. But do you want to? To be known as the American with money? Or do you want to fit in, at least a little?"

I hadn't thought about it, but yeah, I knew what she was trying to tell me. At the lakefront, we came across a stand with tamales and strong dark locally grown coffee. I asked Sam whether we could get some.

"Yes, Joey, I'm not telling you not to spend money. I just want you to think about it. Be aware of the difference between the locals and us. I want to live here a long time. This suits me. I want us to fit in, all right?'

"Okay. Just tell me if I'm doing some big social blunder. But yeah, I'll do my best. Anyway, coffee for you?"

"I'd love some! I'm pretty addicted to it these days, too!"

"You little booger! Getting me worried about sneaking a coffee without you!"

She pushed against me, and then hugged me close. I kissed her quickly. I liked this. Playful and light. And what a phenomenal landscape. Perfect place for a new romance, right?

A handful of locals greeted Sam as we walked. She introduced me to a bunch of her friends, mostly kids and women. Too many names to remember. We sat on the sand with our drinks. To the right of us, some people were washing their clothes in the lake water, slapping the fabric on the rocks to clean them, then wringing them out and laying them on any flat dry surface they could grab.

"They're here every day, washing and chatting and laughing. The tourists come and take photos for a small charge. The women have figured out that if they do laundry here, they get paid! Pretty smart!"

The sun warmed our bodies and even though I was still drained by the long busride and a night making love with Sam, I couldn't take enough of it in. I saw one man and his young kid carrying a bundle on their shoulders, firewood, cut to three-foot lengths and strapped with the same intricate cloth I'd noticed everywhere. The kid had an armful of kindling.

"Most people here cook over open fires in the back yard. It's the man's job to cut the wood every day. The woman makes corn tortillas for hours, and wraps them up for each of the family. Then she comes to wash the change of clothes. The rest of the day is often spent at the market, trading and selling whatever is in season. Avocados. Oranges. Coffee beans are mostly owned by out-of-towners, the farmers are rarely local, more likely to be Ladinos from the cities. That's part of the problem here. The landowners and the workers. Such different lifestyles. Such poverty. This is subsistence living. Basic. Only the basics." She looked me up and down. "Not that you're at all fat, but I bet in six months, those jeans hang off you and you have a woven belt to keep them up!"

I pushed out my stomach as far as possible and smirked.

"Talking of which," she continued, "if we want you to fit in, we need to cut your hair. They don't like the longhaired hippy look. I have some scissors. We can cut it pretty short, like the men around here, and with a hat, you'll blend in all right. Are you worried about that?"

"Kinda, yeah. I hadn't thought it through, but it'll be different for me here, won't it? I have to be more careful. You too, won't you, being with me? "

"We'll be fine, Joey. You know Tom and the men have tons of respect for him. You can help him out with whatever he's up to. Do his work with him and leave the rest to me. And we'll make it clear that we're together, that always helps. Both of us. You can save me from all the suitors knocking on the door when Tom is out of town!"

"Only if I have to!"

I worked. I learned Spanish. I walked. I listened to the men talking. I helped build the new school. Tom and I became good friends, and he treated me as Sam's beloved. If she loved me, then so would her brother. And so I followed Tom's lead.

He took me everywhere. He asked little of me, just that I stick close and quiet. He helped organize the farm laborers. Dangerous for anyone to do at the time. I became his trusted assistant. I kept him safe in a sense, since two of us had more standing than one lone foreigner.

And after two years or so, I wrote. The more time I spent out and about, the more trust I got from everyone in town. So many neighbors talked to me, and they wanted me to tell the world about their lives within the civil war. And it truly was a war. I wrote and sent off photos, articles and essays to the papers in the U.S. I started out utterly ignorant. I learned so much.

I talked to Diego. He lived in San Juan, one of the poorest villages here. The story stunned me. The government had decided they wanted this piece of ocean property on the west coast. The people who lived there were then relocated to the Highlands. They had neither the skills nor the abilities to adapt to a whole new culture. They struggled to grow enough food for themselves. They had their own religion, their own ways of farming, and yes, their own language. The neighboring villages fought them. The kids fought each other. It was a mess. And that doesn't even take into account the brutal politics of the '70s.

"Last month, they killed my grandfather," Diego told me one afternoon.

"Why?"

"Because he wore his traditional clothes. Not western ones like the government demands of us. He died wearing his own clothes. I am proud of him."

I took Spanish classes in Panajachel. Luis was one of the few educated Ladinos who chose to live there. Admittedly, he lived in a small Ladino enclave up in the eastern side of town. I'd walk there with my well-loved pack slung over my shoulder. Young boys followed and chatted to me, asking me questions about where I came from. They didn't believe that I lived in a small adobe home like they did. No electricity, no running water. But I was American! I was supposed to live in a city with all those things advertised in the magazines they sometimes saw. I was supposed to look like the tourists that came for two weeks at a time.

Instead, I was lean, wiry and dark. Sam had won the bet. And now, after three years working and living in Pana with her, I'd become so skinny we'd had to get me new jeans—the belt had made me look ridiculously small and weak. These kids now accepted me, for my carrying wood with them, playing soccer, hauling water and helping out in the school up the road from my home with Sam.

The Spanish lessons were her idea. To make me a fluent, not just conversational, speaker. Another means to the end of making our lives even easier for us, easier to be accepted. We were. To a point. We'd never be anything but foreigners. But they loved us for who we were to them.

And we'd made a home together. So sweet and gentle. Sam amazed me. I'd not known such a comfort with another. So good for me. Sam was so good for me.

Luis told me about his hometown outside Antigua.

"Behind my pueblo is a mountain where the guerrillas live. My village is just outside of Antigua, settled in a steep valley along the only road. Once a week, the guerrillas come down this street, stop all traffic and steal food, clothes, money. They are very quick, maybe fifteen minutes at most. The military always arrives too late to catch them in town. Just outside in the woods the machine guns tear blindly into the hills. My family and I hide under the beds, under the tables and chairs, for an hour."

"Once a week?"

"Yes. Once a week." Luis sipped his glass of water. "Every morning before breakfast or coffee, before going to work, one by one the townspeople walk to the western edge where the city dump is."

"Why?"

"Every day there are bodies. Sometimes it is women, sometimes children, mostly men. We look to see who they have killed."

Walking through the market one Sunday, I stopped to buy some coffee from Miguel at his stand next to the water fountain. We sat and chatted about families. He asked if Samantha was pregnant yet and teased me for not being man enough for her. A tourist bus pulled up, the kind with air conditioning. It was late January or early February and the days were warming up again after a chilly few months. I'd taken a break from following Tom around the villages and enjoyed some time to myself. Sam had gone to visit some English women in San Pedro, and would be gone for few days as it was so far across the lake.

I sat and relaxed. I watched the tourists disembark, so Western-looking. Clean. Pale. Tall, too! Towering over the locals. I sat on the wall and compared myself to them, skinny and tanned, in worn-out clothes, a leather cowboy hat and sunglasses to protect my blue eyes from the intense sunlight.

A couple stepped out. I sat up. The man was well over six feet, dark haired, and obviously well fed. He held out his arm for his friend. She turned to look around and I ducked under my hat.

Kat.

Chapter Seventeen

Still striking with her dark hair tied back, those damn cowboy boots of hers, Kat's shoulders were bare but for the tattoo of a heart. An old-school red heart with the words inside: *I love you.*

I knew that tattoo. I have the same one. On my chest. Above my heart. Done at the same time, the artist worked on us together one summer day in Taos.

Kat. Here. In Panajachel. Why? How did she, well, they end up here?

They walked down the gravel road toward the hostel at the lakefront. I followed. I stood in the doorway and watched them talk to Manuel at the desk. The American man signed in and they followed Manuel upstairs. It was a hotel with only ten rooms, all facing the water and volcanoes. A smart man had built this place: He even had good sheets, or so I was told. Cold water, but it was gravity-fed, unlike most places in town. The tourists loved it. Rustic, but comfortable enough.

I waited. I stood near the women from San Marcos, and their kids kept trying to talk to me, but I brushed them off. Rude. I couldn't help it. I needed to focus. Kat and her friend came out an hour or so later. Kat turned uphill and he walked toward a bar at the end of the beach.

I followed. She walked in and out of the stores, smiling and touching the fabrics. The vendors tried to tempt her to buy their handmade cloth but she shrugged them off and kept walking. She strolled into the bar. My local. Not good. I didn't know what to do. I waited. I watched the front door. I waited. And I walked in.

Kat stood at the window, next to the porch. On the table next to her were two glasses with ice.

I came up to her.

Without turning, she said, "Whiskey?"

"Yes."

"They didn't have Maker's Mark, but it'll do." And she turned to me. She handed me a glass and raised her own. "Here's to my favorite stalker!" and she hugged me tightly.

I sighed and melted into her. "Hi, Kat."

"So what's Sam like? How do you know her?"

I drank back the rest of the whiskey. The bartender came up and introduced himself in halting English and then turned to me and asked, "Donde esta Sam? Y quien es?"

"Es mi prima."

He didn't believe me, I could tell. I'd been warned and I knew that we'd have to keep our hands on the table. I translated for Kat: You're my cousin.

"Kissing cousin?' she'd asked.

I shook my head. "Remember, this is my local. I live here. Everyone knows each other."

"Sam, you mean."

"Yeah. Me and Sam. As a couple. And to answer your question, she's great. We met that summer I rode to California, the year after we met. Played. Anyway, it's so sweet and simple and easy on me. I like her a lot. And we work well together with the kids in the neighborhood. They climb all over me, play games with me, and go running to her for hugs and stories. I love our home, too, the way we've set it up. It's pretty idyllic, really."

"You didn't say you love her."

"I didn't? Really? I do love her, in a way. A deep way." I was quiet.

Kat nudged me with her boot. "So not the romance or passion we had?"

"Past tense. I can't play with you like that anymore. It messes me up too much."

Kat sat back sharply. "I didn't offer."

God, we were like kids, so easily pissed off with the other. Fight. Love. It was never easy for us. Kat ordered more drinks for us, and for once, I let her. I needed to let go for a while, be the rich tourist without a care. So used to being thrifty, it was a pleasure to let her treat us.

"Mark and I live in Denver, pretty big change after New Mexico for so long, but I like it. He has a huge place just outside of town in Boulder, which is a small but creative mountain town. I have a studio nearby that I work in most days. He works for a bank in the city so we see each other at night—all very domestic. I get to try out new materials and styles and have fun on my own, and I love it. And I'm getting a name for myself. Selling new work. Commissions, too. I love it."

"And him? Do you love him?"

"Well, I married him!"

"You did? When? When did that happen?"

"Two years ago. I tried to find you, to invite you, but Paula wouldn't tell me where you were. She told me to leave you alone."

"She did? I didn't know she felt like that." I was pretty surprised to hear that. I'd brought Kat over to the land often enough, and had no clue that Paula was so protective of me. "Did she tell you why?"

Kat looked off sheepishly. "I think she was worried I wanted a last fling with you before getting married."

"Oh. Did you?"

A wicked grin as she turned back to me. "Of course!"

I leaned forward. "We can't do that again. Promise? I can't do that to Sam. She's too good. A good person. I can't do that." Was I trying to reassure myself? Make myself promise? Kat made no such promise.

Manuel from the hotel came by and sat with us for a while. He had a message for Kat. Mark had been back to pick up a coat but was happily out with some musicians, and said not to wait up. Kat kicked me softly. I moved my feet out of range.

Manuel went to the bar and we sat quietly.

"I love Mark," she said. "But it's too domestic, in a way. I'm not attracted to him, don't want him like I used to. And the months keep going by. I want to wake him up. Or is it me I need to wake up?" Kat sounded wistful as she continued. "It's good. Like you said about you and Sam, it's easy. But I don't know how to maintain 'easy' without going crazy. So I go out and flirt at the bar, make out with someone, but that's not enough, either. I tried talking to Mark about it, but he said to get used to 'Married Life.' He said that's what happens, sex changes, and routine kicks in. But I'm not sure how long I can do this, Joey. I need romance. Passion. Sparks flying. Well, you know how it is, or can be. I need that in my life."

I didn't say anything. I lit a smoke and stared out across the railing toward the huge volcano. I couldn't see it, but I knew it was there. I smiled to myself.

"I like my life here. It suits me. But, well, I haven't thought about it until now, but yeah, I guess I liked the drama we had. Crazy fun. I kinda like being calm, though. I need this. Sam is funny in such a direct way. She takes delight in the smiles of the girls when they suddenly get how to read. She's such a great mama. And that's not something I can give her. But she's happy."

"Are you?'

I said nothing.

The sun had gone down, and so had the whiskey. Music kicked in, Garifuna music, a Guatemalan Caribbean mix of salsa and reggae. Kat stood up. "Remember the first time dancing?"

I laughed. "At the end of the night, I told you not to forget!"

"And I haven't! Now let's just dance and play and none of this rehashing and serious stuff. Come on, Joey, dance with me." She held out her hand and I reached for her instinctively. I could do nothing else. Even then.

The lake was dark in front of the porch and we stood near the railing and stepped closer. The bartender turned up the music for us and we danced. We stumbled a few times until we got the rhythm again. Her body leaned into mine. I led. She followed freely. The one place she didn't fight me for control. A beautiful sweet loving dance unfolded. No words necessary. We moved into and away from each other. Smiling. Talking low about silly memories of Santa Fe. A bitter sweetness to every second.

The bar filled up and soon a few other tourists and local men got up and danced around the porch with us. Cutting in on each other, dancing with strangers but aware of where she was at every moment. Laughing aloud in the heat of the music. The night turned into a holiday from home and responsibility. Just what I craved. Freedom to play.

After many hours, and a few too many drinks, Kat asked me to walk her to her hotel. I followed her out the door and down the road. She held my hand tightly. We walked slowly. Silently.

The street was completely empty for once. The stores were shuttered and litter lay on the gravel. I'd never noticed this side of life before. I guess I never came out late at night. Sam wasn't a drinker. Or a dancer. We stayed home.

Near the hotel, Kat pulled me in and kissed me. Roughly. Taking what's hers. I hadn't expected that. I hadn't wanted that.

But I responded. I could never resist her. She tasted just as I remembered. I rocked against her. We bit each other and she laughed as she pushed me and pulled me back and forth. Her hands ran up and down my shoulders and arms. I bit her neck and kissed her clavicle, licking the salty skin

I'd missed so badly. We talked as lovers do, saying all those words that can embarrass when heard by another. Voices quiet, she told me of her love and her desires and then I kissed her softly and tenderly. I wanted to take her, push her against the wall and take her right there, neighbors be damned.

But I stepped back. "I can't do this, Kat. I just can't."

And I walked away. I didn't dare look at her.

I walked home; to the home I shared with Sam.

A few days later, Manuel found me with a note from Kat. He shrugged and told me my cousin had left town but said she'd be back in a few weeks or so.

I thanked him and took the letter inside. At the kitchen table I opened it, a letter from my beloved as I sat in the home of my girlfriend. Messy, I felt messy. But alive. Truly awake.

'Sweet Joey, thanks for another wonderful night. I told Mark about meeting you here. He wasn't too happy about that. But we had great sex finally! Oh, you might not want to hear that part. Sorry. Anyway, we're off to the beaches on the Caribbean coast. Mark has to fly back in ten days. I might stay on. I'll come look for you. I want to meet Sam. Still loving you more and more, K.'

I read it over and over, sealing it into my memory, and then I burned the letter. Did I want them to meet? How would I tell Sam that Kat had found me here? Oh hell, I had to do something. I walked outside and to the market. I took my notebook and wrote to Kat. This was the first time I'd tried to write to her. I stopped and started, tore up pages, ate others. I didn't have the words to explain this, why I wanted this life I had. Or how I wanted her, too. But I couldn't. Couldn't. Wouldn't. Asking her to please let me be. I didn't want to mess this up.

A hand touched my shoulder and I jumped. Papers scattered under foot.

"Joey! I'm sorry; I didn't mean to scare you. You were so lost in your writing. I called out to you when I saw you. I thought you heard me, I thought I heard you say something." Sam looked so upset for scaring me; she stood with her small bag and some flowers from the market. "I thought we'd start celebrating your birthday early, so I got us these. Aren't they beautiful?"

I stood up and hugged her, buried my nose in her shoulder, tried to inhale her, remember her. I wanted Kat gone. And for Sam to take her place in my heart again.

I felt little to be proud of.

"Let's go home. Tell me about your trip. Come on, I'll make us some orange juice."

Sam slipped her arm through mine and we strolled slowly home, with her chatting away and me ignoring my own aching heart.

It was a Sunday morning. My birthday. Sam and I were home. We'd slept in, had eggs and tortillas in bed together. She gave me a book on farming communities. I read. Sam was writing to her parents. Beans cooked on the stove. Someone rapped on the door.

And that simple knock took away my home and my life with Sam. It was all over in that one second. I knew that knock. Those footsteps. I hadn't told Sam yet; I'd thought I had more time.

We had a nice visit. It wasn't that. It's how Sam looked at me after Kat left. It's the fact that Sam walked out. She walked out on me when I wanted to talk to her. Needed to explain. Sam couldn't listen to me. Refused. Her whole energy shifted, from the joy of sharing yet another birthday with me, to one of such horrible heartbreak, I felt like shit. Such an idiot for thinking I had any control, for thinking I could make this life work when I knew I was still besotted by a woman I'd met years before.

I'd been living a lie. And now Sam knew.

For another six months, we lived together. Sam insisted we finish the school projects as we'd promised. After that, she would stay in the house. I would leave. She didn't care where I went. Just to leave her alone. I'd fucked up. I knew it. Sam knew it. Kat didn't. We never spoke after she left Pana. I never did write that letter. It was too late by then. This was my mess.

"Joey?"

"Yeah?" I looked up from the story I was writing about the community gardens. Sam sat opposite me, across the wooden table.

"Look around you."

I did. The small adobe home was full of her paintings and the kids' sketches. She had hung the dried flowers from my birthday. They swung in the breeze through the opening for the window. No glass here, just shutters painted orange. The mud floor was partially covered by a few rugs. The bed was unmade as usual. My change of clothes hung from a screw in the wall. Hers were piled tidily next to her side of the bed.

"Was this just a game to you?" There was no anger left in her. She'd seen me near Kat, and she knew that I had lost myself in another. "Does this mean nothing to you?"

"Oh, Samantha. No. No. You mean so much. You've shown me how to love, to make a home, to relax with you. I never knew such peace…" I faded out. I didn't know what to say, to show her that Kat was the past. "We could stay together. We could. I don't want Kat. I like being here with you. Here."

"Like?" She shook her head. "That's not enough, Joey. That's not enough."

She stood up and poured a glass of water. She sat back down. For once she didn't offer me any. That told me everything.

"You want me to leave?"

85

"Yes, as soon as you're done. The bus leaves at two. You have money?"

Her distance, not cold, but so detached, it froze me, like she'd made the decision and that was that. No more discussion.

"Today?"

"Yes. Today." Sam stood up. "I'm going out to the school for a few hours. I'll go see my brother for a few hours. I'll tell Tom everything. Pack up. Joey, I loved you. I wanted this to last. Us. How stupid of me." She took her books and closed the door behind her.

My hands shook as I drank her water. "I have to leave. I have to leave." I muttered to myself and stood up. "I have to leave. Again."

I looked at our home. "Fuck you, Kat!" I screamed at the walls. "Fuck you for taking this away from me. Fuck You. I hate you. I hate you." My voice broke as I sat back down, crying with my head on the table. "I hate you, Kat."

I packed my few belongings and took the first of many buses on my way back to the U.S. I had to find Kat. I had to find out what this was between us.

And I did.

Chapter Eighteen

"So how shall we do the Thanksgiving? Shall we tell them what's going on?"

I smile weakly. I'm no longer so desperate. The tears had worn me out and now I sit at the table with Paula. We're both exhausted.

"I have no idea. What's worse? To know before you go visit someone that they're dying? Or do I wait till everyone is sitting around the table about to carve a dead turkey and tell them I have cancer, and then ask who likes dark meat? Can't say I've thought about this. Have you?"

Paula actually laughs. "Well, at least you're still funny! No wonder Dr. Nan is so relaxed with this. Now what would I like? If I were the guest? I think some kind of warning. But then again, it's easy for me to talk to my family. You're so much the silent type, no one knows what to expect next. Let's think about that part of it later. Okay, time to make a plan. We only have a few weeks." She tears off a page and starts to write. Lists of vegetables, the name of the farmer with the turkeys, and not forgetting the beer, wine, and kids' drinks. "Who shall we invite? I like Thanksgiving. It'll be great to get everyone around for a week or so."

I relax. I know Paula: She'll bring us a day of joking, with a mix of our family and friends, music, great cooking, all of it. The best gathering possible. Whatever the reason we were getting them here, that didn't matter. She likes to throw a good party. And she does.

If I think about it, Paula has been hiding, quiet, depressed ever since Chris died in the car crash in Santa Fe. This is good for her, too. I like that. This is for both of us.

I make more tea. I look outside and notice the clouds hovering above us. I show Paula and we stand in the doorway, making bets on what time the snow will start and how much we'll have by Thanksgiving. I'm actually getting excited about the idea of a party for us. I tell her exactly that and she turns to me, with her big blue eyes and smile-lined face wrinkled by decades in the sun.

"I like the idea, too. It's been a long time since we all got together like this. It'll be fun. Okay, so more tea, some chocolate, and then we focus."

She tears open a new pack of dark chocolate. Grins and gives me half. She keeps the other half. Neither of us needs to worry about weight! She is still fit and slender, with her mama hips no broader than they ever were. I'm thicker than I was in my sixties but still pretty scrawny by most standards.

We eat the chocolate at the window, racing to finish first. Staring at each other as we chew. Standing. Swallowing. Trying not to choke. Trying not to snort. Paula wins by one square, but then coughs and out it comes.

I claim victory.

Chapter Nineteen

"You knew."

"No, I didn't."

"Yes, you did. I stayed with Paula on my way up here to find you. Maggie loves me. Such a chatty kid. She told me all about you visiting them and how her mama wasn't so nice to you. And how she felt bad so she showed you pictures and postcards and told you stuff to make you smile."

"The postcards on the fridge."

"I wondered. Is that how you found me? Talking to Maggie?"

Kat shrugged with a smile. We both knew at that point. I wouldn't be able to hide from her again.

"And how did you find me?" she asked.

"You'd told me you were living near Boulder. It's still a small place. People know you. I asked. They told me."

I stood on her doorstep. She didn't invite me in. I looked around outside; huge mountains, craggy faces stared down upon us, thick forests crept up to the back garden. Trees surrounded us, held us in their safe embrace. High above us, eagles and ravens flew together. Peaceful, but in a completely different way from New Mexico. I was still adjusting to being back in the U.S.

It had only been a few weeks. I'd stopped in with Paula. As usual, I told her everything. She is someone who brings out the words in me. I told her about Kat and Mark showing up. How it ruined everything. And how when I lost Sam's love, I realized I needed to find out if Kat and I could ever be together. Enough of this on and off crap. Could we be a couple? I'd decided to find her, ask her, demand she make a choice or leave me alone.

Paula sent me off with a basket of food and wine and hugs. She was just glad to have me in the same country again.

"Now what?" Kat stood there still, leaning against the doorframe facing me. Curious.

"Ask me in?" I said.

"I could, but Mark doesn't want you near me. He'll be home soon."

"A glass of wine before he comes back? We could sit outside and talk. I need to talk to you."

She closed the door behind her. I followed her and we walked past my motorcycle. I grabbed the wine and cheese and bread. We headed into the woods to the west. In silence. After five minutes, we came to a meadow full of yellow columbine. She sat down and curled up onto her knees. Again, she just watched me, saying nothing.

I opened my pack, and pulled out my meager picnic. I uncorked the cabernet sauvignon and poured us each a glass. I cut the bread. I unwrapped the cheddar. I offered her a bite.

She held her glass up and nodded. Then asked me, "Are you mad at me for showing up?"

"Yes. I lost everything I'd tried to make with Sam."

"But why? I don't see what that has to do with me! I never said anything to her. We talked about her work. Your writing. The local kids. Nothing naughty. Pretty polite, considering what I could have said. I don't like to share you. And anyway. I never promised you anything, did I?"

I took a drink. Waited to catch my breath. Angry. Intensely angry. "You come and find me. Deliberately. You and I get involved again, even for just one evening. One evening. And then I lose my girlfriend and home and work and life there. I was there for years, pretty damn happy. Then you show up. I lose it all. And you say that it has nothing to do with you? What do you think happened?"

"Oh, we kissed. True. But did Sam know? Did you tell her? I didn't. And anyway, it didn't mean anything, did it? It's just what we do. What's the big deal? Haven't you had an affair before, Joey? Don't be so fucking innocent!"

I stood up and walked off. I kicked at the Gambel oak trees. I threw a rock at the raven laughing in the branches above me.

I looked around. "Am I such an irrelevance to you? A game to play? When your other relationships are crappy, you come to me?"

Kat sipped her wine and ate a chunk of cheese. She lay down, stretched out her arms and sighed. "That's not what I'm saying, Joey. You know better than that. We have fun. We had fun that summer together. Seeing you when I could. A great time with you. But did you ever think we could date? Really date? Fall in love?"

"Yes."

She turned her head and looked at me, surprised. "I mean that much to you?"

"Yes."

I stood next to the tree I'd just kicked. I looked away. Too messed up for her to see me. Too scared to see if she'd push me away again. "Now what?" I asked with my back to her. A whisper, really. I heard the grass under her as she rolled over to face me.

Mid-afternoon sunlight was peeking through the pine trees and the scattered clouds. Birds of all kinds flew around, making spring nests. Snow hid within the higher craggy mountains. Being chilly was good to me after three years or so in Guatemala's gentle climate.

"Come here, Joey."

I did. I lay down next to her. We both rolled onto our sides and stared. Not touching. Not talking. Watching only. Minutes. An hour? I didn't notice. Neither of us knew what to say next. Inevitably, this moment came.

We needed to make a decision. Do we try this? This compelling attraction, is it going to be a driving force for us getting together or is it something to be ignored?

Kat touched my face gently. She caressed my nose, my cheeks, my eyebrows, and followed the lines of my mouth. "Yes," she said finally. "Yes. I'll do this. With you." She sat up and took hold of my hand. We stood. She walked us back to the house. At my bike, she looked at me again. Closely.

"Give me a day. Two. Can you ride to Breckenridge and wait for me? There is a hotel by the river, on the main road. I'll come to you on Friday. I need to talk to Mark."

I couldn't believe it. Her. "Really?"

"Yes, let's try it. Now go, Joey. Give me a couple of days. I'll find you. You know I will. Believe me."

I rode for the afternoon and into the early evening. Mountainous country roads, some were covered with snow piled on the edges, some had fresh sand strewn everywhere. Not an easy drive. I got to Breckenridge by late night. I found the hotel, checked in and lay down on the bed. Ah, shit. Now what? Is this another game of hers? Another time to mess us up? To make me crazy?

We'd tried this briefly. But she was still living with Kelly at the time. An affair. And now? She was married to Mark. And I turned back up. Would she ever be single? At the same time as me?

The year we'd first met, well, we'd snuck around, playing up at Paula's where I lived in the cabin. We'd driven her Land Rover up to Taos for the winter holidays, camped in the back of it with sleeping bags and a small stove to cook on. That Christmas day, she drove me down past Arroyo Hondo and along an incredibly rough road toward the Rio Grande Gorge. We parked at the top. Even her truck wouldn't have made it down and back up with those snowdrifts.

We hiked in. I carried the pack with wine, cheese and bread. Our favorites. At the river, we turned left, and walked to a circle of rocks piled neatly.

"Hot springs. For us alone today," Kat told me as she undressed in front of me, watching me staring at her mesmerized. She stood up, totally naked as the snow came down and rested on her. "You coming?"

I laughed. "Yeah, probably. You too!" I dropped my jeans in a pile and splashed my way into the hot springs to get to her. Laughing, she ducked me under and pushed me against the waterfall. Kat stunned me with her ability to grab me, heart and all. Hours later, and the wine mostly drunk, we talked about our families.

"I hate Christmas," I'd admitted. "Not this one. This is beautiful. The best ever. But no, not my favorite time of year."

"Tell me."

So I did. I'd grown up on a small island in Maine, with my fisherman dad and housewife mom. They'd fought. She drank. He hit her. He killed her. One Christmas Eve. Two days later, he'd drowned. Killed himself. I went to live with relatives in Wisconsin. I was eight. Not good. For any of us.

Kat pulled me into her, wrapped me against her, and kissed me tenderly. Sweetly, and I came undone with this loving.

We'd become far more close after that. Adventures into the mountains. Nights at my cabin. So incredibly close. For more than a year. And she told me stories of growing up spoiled in California, the quiet rage of her mother, the cold demands of her father. An only child, she was always hiding her friends from her family. Ashamed of each other. Unable to be open about what she felt.

But then she'd pushed the door closed to her heart and her body, and told me to leave her alone. That she'd not promised anything. Had been nothing but consistent with me. That nothing was going on. I'd been imagining it, she'd told me. She was in a relationship. With Kelly. Leave me alone, she'd said.

I left. I traveled to Guatemala.

Was I setting myself up again? I had to find out. I stayed in the hotel. I waited. I walked the river, and I hiked the mountains nearby. I drank too much beer every night. Two days. Three days. Four days. How much longer?

On the fifth day she came to me.

Chapter Twenty

Paula suggests we make a list of our favorite people, the ones still alive, that is. We talk about Eleanor, both glad she's not here with me for this. I'm glad she died before I became sick. She loved me too much. I wouldn't want her to live through this. We had such an easy time together. I'm glad I got to hold her for her last breath. I hadn't known I had the strength to be there, but I did.

Paula asks, "Do you want to ask Samantha and her family up here?"

"I don't know. We stay in touch, but I'm not sure whether this is for her. She's so happy in Arizona these days. Kids. Grandkids. I'm happy for her, but it's awkward."

"But that's you. Not her. I reckon we could call and ask if she has plans. Keep it light. She was good for you, Joey. Let's see if she can come. I'd like to see her again. Wouldn't you?"

"Well, yeah. I loved her. Still do, in a way. Okay. Who's calling her, me or you?"

"Me, this time. Who else?" Paula gets up and starts to make a fire. "I have a feeling we'll be here for a while, don't you?" she smiles as she crumples the paper and shoves it into the woodstove beside me.

I roll a cigarette. Now that I no longer care about dying of lung cancer; it's not so strange to smoke again. I like it. It tastes strong, not so nice, but at the same time, I like it. Feels naughty. "Do you still have whiskey around here? Can we have some in our coffee? I'd love to get a bit buzzed right now. Play, you know?"

Paula points to the cupboard to the left of the sink. "In there. I'd like a taste, too, not much but make us fresh coffee and I'll join you. Did you and Tom ever talk after you left Guatemala with your tail between your legs?"

"Yes, quite a bit, really. We wrote letters. I even wrote some articles for him on the Peace Accords of '96, and what was and wasn't working over there. I helped out. He kept the faith in me, seemed not to judge me for hurting his sister. Lucky, you know? He could've hated me. But, no. Admittedly, he doesn't know the whole story. But now he's in Telluride, Colorado, I think. All into bringing back the wolves to the mountains, not popular again! He loves those causes! Gotta love the fella, can hardly walk anymore but has a hell of a mind, fighting mad still."

Paula puts the tea kettle onto the woodstove top. She looks over at me with a question in her eyes.

"Okay, I'll see if he has a chance to come down. I like him a ton. Maybe there's someone driving this way for the holiday? I'll call him. Now who else? Can you get your kids here?"

Paula's eyes suddenly fill and she looks so sad. "I don't know. Maggie will be here, that's for certain. But the boys? I don't know. Mike hardly ever calls these days. And Charlie doesn't like coming back here. Likes San Francisco more than he likes me."

"Oh, Paula. You know that's not true. He's got a full life there, that's all. A home and friends and work and all of it. And that's what you want for him, right?"

Paula's crying as she nods.

"Yes, but…"

"But?" I prod gently.

"I wish he'd talk to me. I don't know what's going on for him, who he loves, if he likes his job, or what he does on the weekends. I feel like he's a stranger. I don't know my own son."

I wait as the kettle heats up. I get the filters from the same shelf they've lived on for over forty years. Paula watches as I pour her a strong coffee and add the whiskey. Maker's Mark. I pour one for myself.

Outside, the snow starts to lightly fall, a white sugaring of the landscape. Paula smiles. "I win the bet!"

I hand her a tissue. "Wipe up, old lady, you're all wet on those wrinkles of yours!"

"You're a fine one to talk. And anyway, I'm only nine months older."

"Oh shit. Did I forget your birthday again?"

"Oh yes, but I don't expect much else from you. It was two days ago. It's okay. Especially now that I know what's been going on for you, Joey."

"Damn it! I wish I could've got that part right. Hang on, I have something for you in the truck—it'll be perfect!"

I throw on my jacket and boots and walk out to the Toyota as fast as I can in the snow. I look back to see if Paula's watching. She's not. I get her a present and head back in.

"Hey, old lady, here you go!" and I throw a sloppy wet snowball into her lap. She squeals and jumps up, laughing hard as she grabs it and lobs it at my head. She gets me good. Snow drips down into my coat and I try to take the thing off quickly, and end up falling against the door. It opens. I fall out into the snow drifting below. I look up to see Paula, crying, cackling and snorting, just as messy as I am.

"You were right! That was perfect, Joey! Absolutely perfect!" She comes down and presses the snowball in my mouth. "If only the kids had been here to see me beat you!"

"So what's it like?"

"What? Eating your snowball? Could do with some salt."

"No! You know, knowing when you're dying? I can't imagine what that's like. Scared to think about it. How is it?"

"Weird. Very weird. Haven't you ever thought about your own death before?"

Paula shakes her head. "No. I can't say I have. I try to avoid the subject. Even with Chris dying like that, and all the funeral stuff afterwards, no, I still tend not to think about it. Denial, I guess."

I sit in the green armchair near the fire. The snow is falling much harder now as I look out the kitchen window, and it's settling all over the piñon trees.

"It's so different this time. The other close calls were a choice. Too much pain for me to deal with. I couldn't see the point. At the time, well, two times, I forgot to watch the clouds. I forgot the ants. I forgot to smell the first cup of coffee in the morning. I forgot how wonderful the warmth of a fire is after a snowball fight. I forgot to notice."

Paula prompts me after a few minutes of silence. "And this time?"

"I've had an incredible life, manic and beautiful and terrifying and demanding and passionate and at times, sweetly easy. Nowadays, I stop and look and laugh and touch and smell and listen and I'm happy. Finally peaceful."

"Are you scared?"

"No, not really. I'm sad. I'm sad to say goodbye to all of this. To all my friends. But, no, I'm not scared. Are you?"

"Yes. I'm scared and sad and worried and not sure how to do this. Sad that I'll lose my best friend." Paula shrugs her shoulders and sips whiskey straight from the bottle. "You'd think I'd be used to you leaving in one way or another. But I'm not. I'm not ready to say goodbye to you, Joey."

Chapter Twenty-One

I'd come back from Tennessee.

I came back to Kat. Back home. To the home I'd built on her land. The home I'd built for us. I loved her. No doubt. She loved me. I knew it. But that didn't mean we could be together. Yet I couldn't let her go. I needed her.

I walked up the drive and knocked on the door. I had my keys but that felt plain rude. I knocked. I waited.

Mark opened the door. "Hello. I was wondering when you'd show up. Come in." I followed him into the kitchen. We sat at the big wooden table. I looked around. Things had definitely changed in the last few months. He had moved in. My touches had gone. The odds and ends of photos taken over the years, all gone. My favorite mug no longer sat on the shelf. My coffee grinder, an old-fashioned one I'd loved, was nowhere to be seen. Details. His details had replaced mine. I didn't want to look in my studio.

"Kat's not here."

"Oh." I didn't know what to say to him. I'd be sarcastic. I wanted to stay clear somehow. "When will she be back?"

"Tomorrow night. She's in Albuquerque for a show. Not my scene, if you wonder. I prefer being home."

"In my home."

"In our home. Kat's and mine. Our home. She's very happy. Glad to be back with me. I'm easy on her, you know? I love her. She loves me."

"I think I've heard something similar, but about me and her." I pull out my tobacco.

"No smoking in here. You can go outside onto the back porch if you need to smoke. I'll get us some tea or coffee. Want some? I think we need to talk before she gets back, don't you?"

I nod and stand up. I step outside and look around. This was my home. I made all of this for my sweetheart. How would I do this? Walk away? I didn't know if I could.

A few minutes later, Mark came out and passed me a mug of black coffee.

"I do love her, Joey. I know this is crap for each of us. But Kat is happy again. She's not shouting at anyone."

"She told you about that?"

He continued. "She is sleeping through the night. No dreams messing her up. She is making some unique sculptures and selling them in all these galleries. She's doing well."

"And she wasn't with me, is that what you're saying?"

"You know I'm right."

I did. But I wasn't going to tell him that. "How's the sex life? Still using the excuse that married means sexless? Not attracted to each other, is that it? You know she likes it rough, right? I can teach you how if you like. She doesn't lie to me about these things."

Mark looked shocked. Hurt. I didn't care.

I carried on. "So, you're telling me to walk away? Because you know her better than I do? Because you're a better man than me? You want me to disappear? And let her think I didn't come back for her?"

He nodded. "Yes, that's best for Kat."

I smoked. I drank the coffee. Good coffee. I didn't speak. I didn't trust myself. After an age of waiting for me to respond, Mark walked inside. I stood and smoked. And thought. What the hell should I do? I didn't know. I sat on the low wall we'd built together around the garden. He was right.

We'd been too much for each other. I'd driven her crazy with my jealousy, my raging fits and those harsh silences. And she'd played games in return. Playing with my head and my lust in equal measure. Come and go. Come and go. Hiding me when I became an inconvenience for her because she wanted someone new.

Her rules, not mine. Never mine.

But I wanted to talk to her. And I knew I shouldn't.

I walked to the west side of the house and looked up at the tile work over the bedroom window. A pattern of blues and reds and yellows, to echo the flowers I'd picked her one day in the Jemez Mountains. The cliffs opposite told me nothing new: Patience. Something I'd never been friends with.

I walked away. I didn't look back. Not this time.

I drove to Taos and found the bar still open. I drank two whiskeys straight up and then a few too many beers. I slept in the truck. Alone.

I drove out north to the Rio Grande Gorge. Kat had brought me here for our first date over six years before. She'd taught me to drive a truck on these flat open gravel roads that linked one side of northern New Mexico to the other, and I'd felt so free and light to be behind the wheel as she chatted and rolled us one smoke after another, telling me about growing up in San Francisco.

This time, though, I parked on the far side of the canyon, and walked back to the middle of the bridge. The gorge was so incredibly deep that the Rio Grande flowed as a stream might in some mountain's open meadow. It was tiny, and silent, the river wandered under my feet. I watched ravens. One or two cars passed me.

One of them parked and out came a happy couple, arm in arm. I listened to the lovers' laughter and my knees buckled and I fell to the ground. They ran over and helped me to a bench. I reassured them it was just vertigo.

"I can see why! That's some six hundred feet of sheer drop. No one would survive that, would they? Look at those rocks and, oh, can you imagine falling like that?" The couple left me after a few minutes.

I walked back to the middle of the bridge. I looked down. Yes, a huge drop. Instant death from something like that. I agreed with the husband's opinion. I stared.

If I can't be with Kat, then can I adore anyone else? What's the point of loving, anyway? If the one who knows me the best can't stand me, then what's the point? I've tried. I've tried to love other women besides her. And I've tried loving Kat. And it's not enough. Mark's right. I'm not good for her.

I stepped onto the edge of the bridge. No cars. I stared up at the clouds and saw nothing. I thought of my parents. Of growing up in homes of strangers. I thought of the home I'd built for Kat. And the life I'd created with Samantha. Paula was my only family. And that's not enough. Not enough to hang my life on.

I stared down at the water some half-mile below.

And I jumped.

Chapter Twenty-Two

I woke up screaming.

In my truck. Out in back of the bar. In my truck, and not falling to my death at the gorge. I was in the truck bed, in my sleeping bag, in Taos. The stars above my head shone unperturbed. I sat up, panting, hearing my own screams as I'd jumped.

The air stirred the cottonwoods next to me and they sounded like the river itself talking to me. I got out of the bag and put my boots on. I needed to walk. I needed to walk. I needed to get moving. My heart slammed and I shook all over. I stared at the stars. I stared at my feet. No one came out after I'd yelled so harshly. No one. Completely alone.

I looked at the truck and turned away. I walked to the plaza. Empty. An untouched town square offered me a seat under more trees facing the old stone and adobe buildings. I sat. I still hadn't uttered the question rattling me into small slivers of heartbreak: *Is this what it's come to?*

I got back to my truck and climbed in. I drove back to our home. No lights. No Land Rover in the driveway. I headed northwest and followed the road toward El Vado reservoir. I crossed the Rio Grande Bridge. I stopped. I parked on the far side of the canyon, and walked back to the middle of the bridge. The gorge was so incredibly deep that the Rio Grande itself flowed as a stream might in some mountain open meadow. It was tiny, and silent, the river wandered under my feet. I watched the ravens. Silence greeted me. No screams. Neither in my head nor out loud.

I drove off. I didn't dare stay there. I might jump.

That wasn't the way.

At El Vado Lake, I stripped off and walked into the dark morning water. I swam out, heading to the other side. Over a mile away, it was beyond me. I'd never make it. I hoped I wouldn't make it. I swam and swam. No tears. No anger. Just one stroke after the next. I swam, focused on the far mountain falling into the water. Freezing cold. Cramps. My legs cramped up. I turned and swam parallel to the shoreline I'd come from. I looked at it and after some time passed, I swam back. I barely made it before my right leg hurt so bad that I cried out. I screamed my impotence. My rage at my own uselessness.

"I can't even fucking kill myself!"

On the sand I lay and sobbed.

The sun overhead woke me. Mid-day. My face had turned hot under the relentless sunshine, red and raw were my arms, my whole naked body sun burned. I curled up.

Finally I stood up and I found my jeans and shirt. I climbed back into the truck. I drove back down the miles and miles of dirt roads. Alone. Badly scared. Shaking. Tears fell and on I drove.

The next day, I found the State Hospital in the city and checked myself in. They didn't doubt me. My belongings no longer were mine. Paula was informed. The psychiatric ward and the locked doors contained my rages. I fought everyone. I attacked my nurses, only to be locked down for days on end. I stared out of the windows. I watched the ravens in the gardens below. I said nothing. Ever.

And it all changed when I had a visitor. Terrified it would be Kat. It wasn't.

Paula had driven down to find me. To hold me. I stared at her before either of us moved and held on tight. She offered me a bag and when I opened it, I found green and blue striped baggy jeans. I laughed in delight. I actually laughed.

"I thought you'd like something other than pink or blue!"

Later that afternoon and with supervision, we walked into the land-scaped park and she and I sat together under a tree. We talked. She held my hand. She understood. And loved me still.

When she left, I asked to talk to my doctor. A few days later, we started working together. Or rather, I started working with him. I wanted to live out in the world. Neither harmful to Kat nor myself. Doctor White listened. Finally someone listened. And I took the first steps to freeing my-self.

Chapter Twenty-Three

"Where were you? Mama told me you'd been in the hospital because of a broken heart." Maggie looked up at me from the front steps, accusatory. "But I know that's not right. That's just your emotions. It doesn't send people to the hospital." She looked more closely at me. "Does it?"

I sat down next to her and stared off at the Ortiz Mountains. The mountains I've loved. I kept coming back, after a few years, I always came back, didn't I? I turned to Maggie.

"You're a young lady now. Well, apart from the scuffed up knees and Mike's overalls, you look all grown up. Are you twelve now?"

She grinned. "Yes! And I turn thirteen in two months. Are you going to be here for my birthday party?"

"Absolutely! What do you want for a present?"

She thought for a moment. "I don't know. I'd like you to make me something. One of your cedar benches or something. Can you do that?"

I nodded. "Yeah. I'm sticking around for a while."

"Were you really in the hospital?"

I nodded again.

"Broken heart?"

I nodded. "But I'm doing much better now. How's *your* heart, Maggie?"

"I like this boy at school. John. He's fourteen already! He just moved to Madrid. They've got an old miners shack on the back road. Have you been there? It was a ghost town. Now, it's changing. It's great. Oscar Huber, the man with the coal mining company, he tried to sell the whole town for something cheap, and no one wanted it. So now his son is selling off the cabins one by one. Mom says it's the artists and hippies and my friends

106

moving in. John and his family live there but I don't go there. I just see him at school. That's all." She smiled sadly. And then perked up. "Are you staying with us again? Please? Or! Or! Why don't you get one of the cabins? Dad wants to buy one and fix it up. We can get two of them next to each other. I'll help! " She stood up. "Come on, Joey. Let's go talk to Dad. Might as well do it now!"

She ran off, still a young'un despite her growth spurts and awkward teenage body. She ran ahead of me, yelling for Chris. I walked slowly. I'd only been out for a week by now. The sights of the blue sky and unending horizon overwhelmed me often and I'd tear up. I walked slowly, smelling the spring air. Funny to be back. Shaky inside myself, but as I walked, I breathed deeply with a smile on my lips. The sun beat down on my pale skin. My body moved quietly these days, unhealthy after a year inside the hospital. I'd done little to stay fit. Hadn't cared about this body of mine till I knew I wanted to live.

But then, I'd made a choice.

I wanted to live.

Chapter Twenty-Four

Paula and I work on the lists for the party. She makes some phone calls and orders the turkey and two ducks from Lisa's Farm in Galisteo. I cook us a green chile stew, with onions, garlic, beef, Serrano chiles, squash and corn. If the snow keeps up, I'll have to leave soon. Drive home. But it's too soon. Telling Paula has drained me. I don't want to leave her yet. The potatoes are cooking on the stove when she looks up at me. "How are you going to tell Maggie?"

I put down the knife and lean against the counter. "I don't know. Would you come with me?"

"Of course. When do you want to talk to her?"

"Tomorrow?"

"Okay, I'll call her and tell her we're coming over for tea. She'll love that. It's going to be rough, though. You know that, right?" Paula puts down her pen and paper. "I'd say telling her and telling Kat will be the hardest on us both."

"Both? Are you going to help me tell everyone?"

She throws her pen at me. "When will you learn, Joey? That's what friends do, they help each other. Jeez! Now give that back!"

I delicately lay it on the table next to her. "Very unladylike of you, Paula. Pass things to me, not lob them, next time. Hey, where's the cumin? I'd like to add a touch in the onions."

"Top shelf by the window. All the herbs stay there these days. And I have some cilantro in the greenhouse. Want me to get some?"

She comes back in with a light sprinkling of snow in her grey hair. She hands me the cilantro and a few lettuce leaves for a salad. "I think you should head home after we eat, okay? Before the road gets icy."

I nod, she's right. A night at home is a good idea. We've spent the afternoon here together. Maybe I'll be okay at home now? I ask her if she's all right and she smiles at me. That's that, then.

We eat. The whiskey had made us sleepy but the food gives me energy. I chat about how we'd worked on the miners' shacks in Madrid. And how much fun it was to tear them apart and put down fresh lumber, making me a bedroom in a loft like I love. She reminded me of Maggie painting all the window frames with John, her first and only love. They'd found a bunch of half-used cans of all the colors possible. My home was a little happy bright spot in the lingering sadness. As my home came together, so did my spirits. I'd laughed again. Paula had fed me. Maggie had spoiled me with her stories and by bringing her friends to plant in the new vegetable garden out back.

"And then, working with the boys and Chris next door. Charlie and I reading for hours on end outside on the new wooden decks, chatting about his friends and mine, and how difficult it all seemed to get to know anyone, even to him as a teenager. We all grew up together. Kept the family spirit alive by working and playing. How amazing was that? What a summer. What a year. Chris was a great man, Paula. You had a keeper, eh? I'm glad you guys stayed together all that time. He was such a good man."

Paula smiles. "He was. He loved working on all those projects with you. I'd hear him chatting away and every now and again, you'd laugh out loud, snorting, too! The boys would follow you two around like puppies."

"It didn't take them long to be the ones with all the great ideas. No wonder Charlie is doing so well in San Francisco, all those remodel jobs. We taught him well! I'm looking forward to talking to him again. It's been too long."

"I'll call him tonight. You're right. He's busy. Always was private about his life, wasn't he? That's okay. I'll talk to him. Invite him. And if he's not sounding too positive about coming out here, can I tell him?"

"Yes, tell him I need to talk to him. You can tell him why, if you need. Well. Think I'll go. Did you need to throw anything else at me before I go?" She grins and picks up her soup bowl.

"Hey! I was joking!"

"Me, too. Now get back to Fred and the cats. Stay warm, Joey. Come over in the morning."

We both just look at each other. No words needed. I smile softly. And I leave, for the night.

Chapter Twenty-Five

"My family's been here since 1896—did you know that? They worked in Cerrillos. The mines. It was such a bustling town! You'd never think so now, would you? I heard all these stories of the number of bars and brothels and trains and mining deaths. Yes, I look at the five streets left and imagine the way it used to be, with two or three thousand folks working and drinking and fighting. And then, for me? So damn sleepy. I'd always wished I'd been around then instead, too damn quiet when I was a kid." Chris passed me the hammer and nails. "Pound in those corner pieces and then we can take a break before the boys get off from school."

I reached over and took the supplies from him and turned to the loft bed we were building. We'd put in a window last week, one that faced east, for the morning light. I needed brightness. As much as possible. Chris suggested a skylight above the bed. I worked silently as Chris cut more two-by-fours for us.

"I reckon we'll be done by tomorrow afternoon. At least the bed'll be ready for you. Want to stay in here this weekend? It's doable, you know."

Chris always chatted away, and never pried. Talked but rarely demanded much back from me. Easy company. And I laughed at the right time, apparently. He enjoyed us working together. Last month we'd closed up his miner's cabin next door. It took ages to fix the holes in his roof but that was now taken care of. He'd wanted us to set up my home for fall and winter. Give me my own home. And in the spring, we hoped to work more on the floors and to install some kind of plumbing into his. For his kids, that was his goal. Charlie was a teenager, and so damn handy that Chris thought to do the basics first, and then let Charlie play with it after that. Conditional on there being a place for Mike, for when he wanted to move out to Madrid. Away from his mom and dad.

In my own head, I figured I'd give Mike my place if I left town again. He could live in it for me.

I'd always wanted to have a son. A kid. I couldn't see it happening now. Too messed up. But here was a kid who might love having his own place. If I leave again, that is.

"Do you want to bring in the furniture on Friday? I could get Charlie to drive my blue truck for us, and we can get it all down here in one afternoon. Of course, we'll have to give Mike a job to do, too. But then we get to have a housewarming that night, right?"

"Right! I'll cook for you all!"

Chris laughed. "How about we ask little Miss Maggie to fix up something? Her and John will probably show up, anyway. A gathering in your new home, that sounds pretty good."

I grinned. "I'd love that. Just what I needed. A new sweet place. And I can write over here. This window is the best height for a desk and a chair. It'll be so calm, to look out at you three working next door while I sit here with my coffee!"

Chris laughed as he put his tools on the worktable beside him.

I climbed down the ladder. "Break, boss?"

"Yep, five minutes! And when the rest of my family gets here, let's get them to help us lift these boards up onto the framing. Make it ready for us to finish in the morning. Anything else?"

"Not that I can think of. Should be warm enough in winter with that woodstove. I'll need to go to cut firewood in the next few months. Oh, and when do we need to get back to watering your stuff? How's it all looking up there?"

"Good. It'll be a good harvest. That'll help. The rains helped. But maybe on Sunday you can work up there for a half a day or something. Check on it. I'll be out with the family in Pecos for the afternoon."

"Sounds fine. Come on, then, let's get ready for those kids of yours."

Chapter Twenty-Six

I wake up laughing.

We'd had such a wild night for the housewarming. Mike, the scrawny teenager, a wild boy by then, had climbed up onto my roof and hung my socks, to air them out, saying they stank. Charlie fixed up the lights to brighten the loft bedroom for me, making it as cozy as possible. Maggie and John had brought over some cookies his mom had made for us. Paula had lentil stew, wanting us to eat something good since she knew we'd all be smoking and drinking beer soon enough.

The stories that came out were hilarious. I finally told on Paula's chasing the boys in Chicago. She told on me fire-breathing at the beach, with a can of stolen gas and sticks and string. And how I'd set my hair on fire and that she'd thrown her beer over my head. I'd gotten pissed at her because I hadn't realized I was on fire! Chris admitted to stealing a keg from the local bar that same party on the beach, wanting to get Paula alone and giggly.

The kids started telling on each other and we heard about school mischief and instead of any more 'Mom-Moments,' Paula looked over at me, saw how my eyes were lit up in pure comfort and laughter. She kept quiet and told more stories about being an idealistic rebel hippy chick in the city, trying to grow food in the empty lots by her church. And getting in trouble for growing carrots instead of pot!

Finally, it was time for them to all leave. Their hugs and jokes echoed in the rafters after they'd driven off. They gave me my first night full of the sweetest energy. A family home, that's how it had felt. And that's what it became. Busy. Loving. Full of people's laughter echoing in the rafters long after they left me alone. Alone but never lonely.

I climb out of bed, full of such happy dreams.

Freezing, it's damn cold in here. I look out the window and I can barely make out the juniper on the doorstep. The snow is drifting and sweeping in and out of every branch. I check on the stove and throw in some more piñon and oak. I light a lamp and sit back in bed. I love my home. Fred snores at my feet. The cats come on over since I'd woken them up. Both on my lap.

I listen to the flames and the wind. Beautiful. Absolutely beautiful.

Chapter Twenty-Seven

That first date with Kat, 1967, the first real date, outside of her bedroom, was so incredibly beautiful. Yeah, I'm a romantic, sappy as a humid sock. I had asked her to take me to the Jemez Mountains. I'd been staring at them for months but had never been out there. We'd been having an affair for some six months by then, but our time had been contained to the sheets that tangled us. She loved the idea of a day out together. She drove to Cerrillos and met me by the railroad tracks. We left my motorbike parked off to the side of the dirt road.

"This way. It's pretty rough along this road, but there are tons of stories down here. I'll keep you entertained as I drive. Can you roll me a cigarette? I kinda like them now. Anyway, how was your morning?"

I told her of waking to Maggie and the boys outside my cabin door, chanting, "Joey has a date! Joey can't be late!" Over and over. They'd heard their mom and dad talking about it over breakfast. The kids brought me coffee and told me to hurry up and do my chores.

"Which are?"

"Watering the plants in the greenhouse and feeding the new chickens."

I told about how Maggie had named each of the eight new hens and the boys called the roosters Big Ben and Big Bill.

We drove through the arroyo and along the railroad tracks toward the west. The sun, as usual, was perfect, warming and bright. I was still getting used to the weather in New Mexico. I'd become pretty dark-skinned within these first two months, from working outside with Chris and Paula.

Kat rolled down her window and tapped the ash outside. "I finished the self-portrait last night. Stayed up till one or two, probably, with the finish details. The oil sealer and the wood stains. Looks damn good, I reckon. I like it. A lot. Not sure what to do with it. I can't imagine trying to sell a sculpture of myself in the nude!"

"I'd buy it!"

She glanced over. "Yeah, you probably would, wouldn't you? Maybe I'll just keep it for when you're rich! Hey, did you write about the bike ride across country? I think I know where you could send it to get published."

We talked and talked about our different creative projects, challenging the other to follow the dreams through, not just blather on about things.

To be honest, I think that's what we loved in each other from the beginning, that we're not dreamers but doers. Productive in weird off-beat ways. I loved finding out what she was working on. Kat always asked after the latest writings I'd done since the time before. Funny. We could be in the middle of making out or sexing each other when she'd stop me to get the updates. Made me laugh every time, her direct and blunt interest in who I am, what I'm doing. However bad her timing, I'd stop, answer and then get back to the task at hand.

Along the road were broken-down stone buildings and half-crumbled mines.

"For a long time Waldo, here, was the center of the turquoise mining in the Southwest. The place dates back to the mid-1800s. Isn't that unbelievable? The town itself fed and housed and boozed up thousands of workers. A train track was built for Madrid alone, for the coalmines there. They almost made Cerrillos the state capitol!"

"That's crazy! No one lives there now. It's so quiet. Well, there's Mary's bar! Was that there then?"

"No idea. We could ask on our way home, stop for a drink. Up ahead is where the road drops into Cochiti, an Indian pueblo, or reservation, not sure which it is. But we're driving up through there and up this intense dirt track into the hidden side of the Jemez. I haven't done this before, but I saw a line on a map and figure we can make it with the Land Rover. If I get tired, can you take over?"

I giggled. "Nope. I don't know how to drive!"

She looked over at me, shocked. "Really?"

I nodded. And laughed again. "It's up to you today. I'm here as a passenger this time. All yours, Kat!"

She shook her head. "I don't think so. Once we get to the main road on the other side, I'll teach you how. Just start watching me change gears and all that. I'm not into babying you, Joey. It's time you learned."

I smiled. "Okay, then I get to teach you to ride the motorbike. Tomorrow soon enough?"

She shook her head. "Wrong again. Being on the back of the bike is the only time I like to give it up, let you take control. All right?" She had a wicked grin as she said that. I reached over for her.

We drove and drove. The sun hung high behind us at this point. I passed her some nuts and fruit from Paula's kitchen. We chatted and laughed. We drove in silence, too. The hours passed easily and sweetly.

Such a romantic adventure up through the thick mountainous forests. The road became almost impassable. I had to climb out to haul off a few trees that had fallen and closed off passage. I sat and stared out across huge canyons and deep into the valleys and cliffs and caves that surrounded us. Kat stayed quiet for a while. Deep in her own thoughts. She concentrated. And once we had reached the highest point with the unbelievable views over toward Santa Fe, she stopped the truck.

She climbed out and held out her hand. I took it. I followed her to the rocks that made a wide flat table. She stood in front of me. She reached for me and undid my shirt. She took off my jeans and my boots. I stood naked before her. She looked me up and down. She reached out for my hand again and rested it on her breasts. She turned from me and stared into the distance.

"What's wrong, Kat? Are you okay?"

She held my hand to her still and shook her head. "I'm scared of this, Joey. It's too good. Too good to be true. Too good for me. I can't do this."

I turned her back to me and kissed her.

She held me to her. And then sighed. "Let's go. I heard about some hot springs around here—let's soak, okay? Come, sweetheart. Get dressed!"

We found a meadow just half an hour later, with a small waterfall. We climbed the falls. In our eagerness to see what was on the other side, we forgot to take our clothes off first. Soaked—surprise, eh? She laughed as we took everything off and lay it on the rocks to dry. We made love. I poured us wine and gave us some snacks when the munchies hit afterwards. She sprawled in the grass. Relaxed and rejuvenated. Kat fell asleep in the midday sunshine. I watched her breathe. For two hours, I just watched the woman I loved.

She stirred and told me that she couldn't be with me. That she was with Kelly. But that she wanted more. And couldn't. She turned to me, sadly.

We reached for each other anyway.

Later that day, we drove south, that is, once we hit the main road that headed toward the Jemez Springs. Off the side of the road she found a parking space with no one but us. She took out the towels from her bag and asked me to carry the water bottle. We climbed down a steep and rocky half-hidden path. Balancing carefully as you walked the tree trunk was the only way to get to the other side of the river. Then we had another steep climb upwards.

After ten minutes of silence, Kat turned to me and grinned. "Bath time, Joey. Hot springs for us. And only us today. Come with me."

"Oh, I plan to!"

I grabbed her against me and started to take her shirt off her. Pulling it up and over her as she half-heartedly fought me. I got it free. I touched her belly button. And she smiled at me so broadly. A huge happy smile of unedited enjoyment. It was rare and wonderfully amazing to me each time I saw this freedom in her.

That smile of hers was my undoing.

Chapter Twenty-Eight

I open the trunk and reach in. The first thing I find is my birth certificate. Not a good memory. Mike and I had a huge fight last time I saw him. Because of it. I'll have to talk to him when he comes. I want to explain. I need to talk to him.

Underneath that, I find some photos. Of the kids growing up in the hills. Of Sam and Tom and me on the lakeside in Guatemala. Of Rian and me in Valencia on the back of a truck, driving through the orange groves. I looked so happy and relaxed with her. She was a teacher at this school in Valencia, Spain. I'd met her in my forties. I'd gone to Europe for a while. You can imagine why, I'm sure.

So, yes, I was traveling through Spain. It was pretty old-fashioned, rough roads, not much modernization at that point. I'd wanted to clean up again. Internally. Externally. I'd found a small place to rent near the ocean in Valencia. I'd hitched through the country for about six months by that time.

I met Rian shortly after coming to the city. I taught English. She signed up. For more than language lessons.

This photo comes from the trip we took up to Madrid to meet her family. She'd wanted to take the train. I'd suggested an adventure, hitching with the farmers heading north through the desert. She agreed. We hung on to the sacks of fruit. We chatted about Spain. She'd wanted me to understand the country and the people. The music is what caught me. Laughing with her is what caught our hearts.

Fun memories. Fun and silly. Those three years together kept us both smiling, even at the inevitable end. She laughed easily and so did I. I left with a smile in my heart and hug from her and her whole family. A bittersweet smile.

What else? Ah. Some books. Kahlil Gibran. Such simple wisdom. It suddenly occurs to me: I'd like Charlie to have my books. Charlie would be perfect. His homes are always full of books, friends and stories. And that's what we shared, a love of the written word. Yes, I want to give him my library. I have the classics from Europe, the German writers, like Thomas Mann, Heine, Durrenmatt, too. A few Spanish writers and playwrights like Lorca that I had started to read this last year. And then there is the old school English literary background I'd disliked for many years. Now, though, I read these books by the Bronte sisters, Dickens, and the plays of Shakespeare. I try to discover for myself why these works have lasted decades, try to understand the beauty of their words. Maybe Charlie has the answer? I still don't.

Kahlil Gibran's book came to me when I was last in Maine. Visiting a relative, someone I'd stayed with for a few years as a kid. Maybe when I was twelve or something. An aunt. Not by blood. Not close but still, she'd helped me, housed me. And during that visit as adults, we'd run out of things to say to each other, but then she gave me this book and a hug. And wished me well. I'd been in my late fifties. I'd come back from England with Eleanor. I was different. Softer. And I'd hugged my aunt and thanked her. For everything.

Maggie, though. I really want to find something extraordinarily precious for her. She has always been my special sweet young friend. Despite her tendency to constantly tell Kat where to find me!

What can I give her? My map of the world? The postcards she showed Kat every few years? The letters she'd written me? The photographs? I need to think this through. What would mean the most to her?

I get up out of the armchair and put on the water for my first cup of coffee. The pets sleep on. The fire smolders. The snow falls. I stand at my kitchen window. I have a full day ahead of me. I don't need to find the perfect present right now. I have a couple of weeks till the party.

A party! What a concept! I like the idea. I really do. I'm a little worried about telling them all why we wanted them here with us. And I'm still not sure about talking to Kat. I can write to her, perhaps? No. Paula won't let me do something so stupid! I can hear her now, telling me off: 'Either I talk to her, or don't contact her at all.' She's right. I couldn't tell her this stuff on paper. That would be cruel.

But cruel suits us, too.

I wait for the kettle to whistle. The filter is ready and waiting, balanced on top of the green and yellow stripy mug. I still take it black with a teaspoon of honey. It's good for me like this. Not too sweet. And cream just goes off too fast for me. I don't like shopping more than once a week these days; Santa Fe is too huge. Where I remember open fields, prairie dogs and arroyos, now I see malls, big box stores and parking lots. Not my idea of fun or beauty.

The kettle boils. I pour the water, wait and have my coffee.

It's simple, the pleasure I take in the smells, the taste, the warm mug in my hands. I sit back at the stove and watch some wood catch fire and burn. The crackle of the flames. The steam of my drink.

Outside it continues to snow.

Chapter Twenty-Nine

"I have this for you." I hand Maggie a photo of the two of us on my front steps in Madrid.

"You were twelve or thirteen, I think."

Maggie laughs. "Look at those skinny legs of yours! And is that Jimmy behind me? It looks like him. My, oh my, look at us!"

"Funny, eh? Probably late '70s, is my guess. And look at your t-shirt, Mickey Mouse! Hollywood comes to Madrid!"

Maggie laughs at the thought, and passes the photo to her mom.

Paula had seen it on the way over. We'd laughed about how I'd ended up staying. How she'd tricked me into taking on a pregnant dog, Angel, and had ended up keeping one of the puppies. I'd loved Jimmy the most— he was my first dog. He came everywhere with me. I chatted to him all the time, more than with any humans I knew. Personally, I think Paula was a tad jealous! Anyway, I stayed. I'd bought a house on Back Road. I'd settled. Maggie's crush that first summer became her first love. And, my crush came back to haunt me yet again.

After two or three years in peace, Maggie came running up the road one afternoon.

"Kat's here! Kat's here!"

I stopped writing.

"Where?" Jimmy sat at my feet. He looked up and wagged to see his playmate.

"Her and some man, they're moving into the yellow house down by the Mine Shaft Tavern, making a gallery or something. I talked to her and told her you were here. That we got you to settle down! She seemed happy to know where to find you. Her boyfriend was grumpy. Are you going to see her?"

Now a fifteen-year-old, Maggie was a complete romantic as far as Kat and I went, more so now since she had a steady boyfriend.

I shook my head.

"I bet she comes find you! Twenty cents I bet."

Maggie sat on the steps and we looked down the road. We could just see the house where Kat and Mark were moving into. I saw her Land Rover off to the side. Lots of activity down there.

"Where's John?"

At home, she told me. And then she walked into the kitchen and opened cupboards.

"I'm hungry, got any cookies? I have to go see Charlie and Mike, but I wanted you to know she was here. Are you happy about that? You still love her, right?"

"Yeah, but it's complicated. Not so clear-cut as that. But you know that, Maggie. She and I don't do so well together."

"But it's love! That's all that matters, Joey. Love is great!" and then she'd blushed.

I didn't tease her too much, then or now.

Later that month, Kat had come to find me. I'd kept my distance till then. She walked up Back Road toward me, her head down against the sun on her face. She didn't know I was watching her. My knees went weak and I sat on the rock steps, only a few hundred feet from her. She had dyed her hair, more reddish than pure black, tied back in a ponytail. She wore flared blue jeans with black stripes along the sides, matching her jacket. Black and red cowboy boots. She looked up. And grinned wickedly. "Got any Maker's Mark for us?"

And she reached out her hand to me. I took it. And I led her inside, closing the door behind us.

Nothing had changed. Not enough.

Once in the kitchen, I opened the cupboard where I kept the wine, beer and whiskey. I didn't drink too much myself at the time. Better to keep sober, that's what my doctors said. So I did what they suggested.

Kat sat at the table and looked around, assessing my home. "I like it, very much your style. Reminds me of our home up north. I like the loft, the way you did the stairs—it's beautiful, Joey. And you put up some of those old photos! I'm glad." She stood up and went to the shelves by the woodstove and picked up one of the two of us with my bike behind us. "Remember when I gave that to you? I think you were about to go to Tennessee and I didn't want you to forget me."

"Even though you were leaving me for Mark? Even though you wanted me gone?" I couldn't help myself. I had to give her shit. "Well. It worked out for you then, eh? Still together?"

She nodded, glanced over and looked away. She seemed uncomfortable, kept pacing around. I made her uncomfortable. I liked realizing that. I waited. Kept quiet. Finally she came back to the table and sat back down. She took the glass and raised it in a toast. "To my favorite stalker!"

I didn't drink. I watched, curious as to what had prompted her to find me this time.

"I was joking, Joey! Honest!" She put her glass back down. "Are you doing better these days?'

"You heard?"

Kat nodded again, this time clearly not liking this distance. I hadn't reached for her, had put the table between us and not said much, as yet. I didn't trust myself to speak to her. I'd be mean and what's the point of that?

"How's your heart?" she asked me, and then I knew.

I nodded. "Maggie?"

"Yes, who else tells me these things?"

I laughed quietly and explained it's even worse now that Maggie had found her true love. Romantic to the core. And John didn't discourage her, either. "What else did she tell you? By the way, you owe me twenty cents. She bet you'd come up here."

Jimmy came over and sat at Kat's feet, staring, tail slightly wagging. She reached down to pet his ears and then he rolled over, belly up for her, a stranger in my home. Great guard dog, eh? Kat knelt down and played with him a while. No words between us.

I got up and started dinner, rice and veggies from the gardens. I'd started to grow my own greens now. The evening came upon us. Kat was playing with the two dogs, and I was cooking. We were quite domestic, more than I'd wanted. I didn't want to start the much-needed conversation, though. I kept quiet.

Eventually, Kat came over and leaned on the table near me.

"Can you get two bowls from that shelf?" I asked her.

She watched me stir the food one last time before I served us both.

I gave her the two bowls, and walked outside. I needed some air, to be alone for a second. She didn't follow me. Jimmy did. We stood on the steps and I looked around. Her house was dark, no lights on. Was Mark away? I came back inside and joined her and began to eat. She started it.

"How come you're so quiet? Don't you have anything to say to me? Ask me? Tell me?"

I stared at her. "How fucking arrogant, Kat! I go through hell and then, when it suits you, you come find me. Expect me to talk to you like I used to?" I laughed, bitter and cold. "Have another fight with Mark? Or don't you two fight? Too bored with each other?"

Kat stopped eating. Leaned back in her chair. "That's better. Let it out."

"Fuck you."

Impasse.

Neither of us would budge an inch nor would she leave, except on her terms.

After half an hour or so, Kat shrugged. "Mark and I have a good thing going on. It suits me. He leaves me alone a lot. He has his own friends in Santa Fe. He works in the city, too. We like each other. It's enough. For now. I'm not looking to start anything with you, Joey. We can't go back."

"Damn right. And I'm not interested. I don't know why you're here, though. Why stir it up again? And why the hell did you move to Madrid? I like being here. I don't want you around me. Messes me up." There, I'd said it. Got it out. And without a fight.

Kat just looked at me. She stood up and put her bowl in the sink. "I'm sorry, Joey. I loved you. I still do."

And with that, she left.

She left me alone for a while. She'd dropped off the sculpture she'd made all those years before.

"A housewarming gift," she'd said. It was a lifelike nude of her kneeling, with her head tilted as if listening to me. I put it in the bedroom. After that, we stayed away from each other for months.

But then we bumped into each other one weekend at the tavern.

One Friday night and it all came back. A band was playing. I'd worked hard all day with Chris and the two of us were relaxing with a few brews. I've always loved sitting at the bar with him, chatting away, laughing and teasing. Charlie was out, too, hanging out with his friends on the porch. Chris had some work coming up, out of town, and he needed my help on the farm, for me to help Paula out most days. I promised to be there with her as much as she needed, with the kids, the plants and the various chickens and goats they now had. A regular homestead. I loved being up there. We'd even built a studio for them, a simple wooden structure that took us a week to erect. Not bad, eh? We talked about the cabins and the odds and ends we both wanted to get done before it snowed too much. After a couple of beers, Chris yawned and made his goodbyes, leaving me there to walk home later. I watched the band, not really my style, but danceable rock and country.

"Whiskey, please."

I recognized her voice over the music. She looked at me, smiled, and asked if she could sit with me.

"Okay. How's business?"

Kat told me about the work she was doing there, the new black and white paintings she'd discovered she loved doing late at night. "When there are less distractions, a limited visual stimulus, I sit in the studio with a candle and the moonlight and then I paint."

"What kind of things?"

"It's abstract; for anyone else, it wouldn't make sense. But I see people and the rooms I imagine them living in. It comes to me, with these very strange images and pretty dark emotions. Not easy to explain. I've got to say, I love painting nowadays."

"No sculptures?"

Kat shook her head. "Not recently. I still have a bunch to sell, but nothing new. And you, Joey? What are you working on?"

I ordered one last beer and turned back to her. "Nothing creative. I tried writing when I came out of the hospital, but I couldn't stand what I wrote. So I burned it all. Now, it's the home. I like playing in there, tile work in my kitchen for now. In the spring, I want to make a stone garden and a shady area to sit in. I'd love some columbines and native stuff like that, so I've been collecting seeds like crazy. I still write articles every now and then. I work with Chris, mostly. Help out with Paula and the farm. She's still up there, you know."

The two of us caught up, chatting pretty easily, no tension, no flirting for once. I relaxed. She chatted and made me laugh. I let my guard down.

"Dance with me, Joey?" she stood up with her hand out to me. I reached for her.

"Sure. Just one. Then I should go."

We danced for the next three hours. A few stumbles and squashed toes to start. No longer talking much. Laughing occasionally. Her body relaxed into mine and we found our rhythm. We melted against each other. And became as we were.

For more than two years, we danced together. At the bar. In my home. Out in the mountains. Whenever we wanted the other to come to us, we left a message with the one word, *dance?* And we did. Literally.

We found little known places all over New Mexico, where we wouldn't meet anyone she knew, and we'd spend the night, dancing and laughing and talking the sweetest nothings. No drama. Easy. Loving. The taste of her skin on my tongue. Playing games and coming and going in the middle of the nights. We had an unbelievable time, full and satiating.

Yes, an affair. No, Mark didn't know. Paula did, though. She wasn't happy for me. She told me over and over, so after the first few months, I cut her out of my life. I worked with Chris. I told him little. Maggie saw, though. She knew. And she kept quiet about it.

One night at the Mine Shaft, Kat found me in the parking lot, sobbing in the corner under the trees, curled up on the dirt. I couldn't do this anymore. The disconnection we had between the private and the public. She'd feed my heart with all her private attention, affection, and the passion that we shared. Full of love and laughter. And then for me to compare that to the public coldness, this indifference of hers, it broke me.

I fell apart one night. One weekend night. Clear as day, I see myself, broken and destroyed by the changes in her moods. The inconsistencies. I didn't want to hide my feelings for Kat. Yet, she wouldn't talk to me when we were out and about. Only on her terms. Hidden. Quiet. An affair. One that she directed. She saw me that night, humiliated by my own anguish. And it broke me.

That one photo brought it all back. I shake myself, only to find Maggie and Paula watching me. Paula stands up to make us tea. She goes into the kitchen and shuts the door.

"Maggie. I have some bad news."

She leans back in her armchair. "Okay. What is it?"

I tell her. She simply sits there, and looks away briefly. Then she turns back to me and asks, "How can I help?"

"That's it?"

She smiles sweetly, as she always has for me. "You wanted tears and sobbing and tearing out my hair?"

"Well, yes! Paula said you'd be the hardest to tell. But you're the easiest!"

"How many people have you told?"

I grin. "You and your mom!'

Maggie laughs in delight. But she then turns serious. "I'm sorry for you, Joey. But it's okay. I lost Anne when she was only two. And Dad last year. A few friends, too. And anyway, I thought I'd lost you a few times there. So I'm just glad you stuck around for so long. You were always my sweetest friend. I told you everything when I was kid, didn't I? And I've loved you ever since I was three years old. That not a bad run, is it?"

Paula comes back in with a tray of goodies. Tea in three huge blue mugs. A plate piled with cookies and a cake. With a candle, already lit.

"A late birthday celebration for me. Less about you, Joey! Back to me. I heard you laugh, Maggie, so I knew I could raid your fridge, that you weren't too upset!"

Maggie looks at me. "I bet twenty cents that you forgot her birthday again. You did, didn't you?"

Paula and I exchange a look and then tell her about the snowball fight we'd had in the kitchen. I hand over the twenty cents.

We sing Paula *Happy Birthday*, eat cake and relax. The snow has stopped falling. The sky clears up and I suggest a walk in the dog park. Not that any of us has dogs with us. Fred is home, curled up on my bed, probably, with two cats leaning on him to keep warm. I just like the idea of us being outside.

Maggie drives us over there. Not many people, but we sit on the bench and chat. No other big news but for my health. We tell her about the hope for a Thanksgiving party.

"Like a going-away party! I like the idea. When we get home, let's play with it all and get it coming together. And after all of that is sorted out, tell me about the cancer and what you need from us. Does David know?"

"I wanted to talk to you first, but next time he comes over, I'll talk to him. How's his love life with Jamie? Are they back together?"

"Oh, yes. He's pretty much in love. And I think she is, too, but she's taking it more slowly than he'd like."

"Kind of like with you and John, then?"

Maggie laughs. "I just pretended not to be in love."

"Well, she didn't fool us, did she?" and Paula hugs her daughter to her. And then passes me a snowball behind Maggie's back. We attack her at the same time and she screams in surprise, and pushes me off the bench into a two-foot drift. Paula giggles so hard, she almost joins me on the ground. Maggie runs back to the car. And locks us out.

"Will you two behave? Are you sure?"

We nod as we stand at the locked doors, looking in at her sitting in the heat, engine running.

"Promise?"

Paula and I ignore each other and nod like naughty kids. Seventy-one-year-old kids.

"We promise!"

Back at the house on Baca Street, Maggie turns up the heat and we hang out our wet clothes. Tea is made. Knees rest. We sit in the living room, the one that overlooks the arroyo and the cottonwoods. We sit quietly, not needing to talk, not yet.

"What's the plan? Is Mike coming home? Or Charlie? I'd love to meet Mike's new girlfriend; she sounds like a riot when we chat on the phone. She makes him laugh so much, that's what he tells me. Have you talked to him, Joey?"

I reluctantly tell them both that Mike and I had a huge blowout two years ago.

"At Eleanor's funeral?"

"A few months later."

"Why?"

It's a question I'd been dreading, but I simply say how we'd shouted at each other. Said some things. I felt bad for not going into any details but I couldn't without talking to him first. Maggie and Paula look at each other, and then one of them asks me, Is that why he hasn't been back?

"It could be. I know I wasn't so nice to him. Told him to keep quiet."

"Well, what's so important to fight over? That's unlike you two."

I can't answer them. I just shake my head and ask for the next topic. There's an awkward few minutes of silence and then Paula pulls out her bag and from there, the lists. Her infamous lists! Maggie takes one and reads through it quickly.

"How about we set up who calls which one? I'll talk to Mike. You can call Charlie, Mom. He'd like that. And you call Kat."

"No. I can't. I don't want her to know."

Maggie puts down the paper. "But Joey, you still love her, right?"

I nod.

"Well, you need to tell her. She has a right to know, to come back to you if she can. Right, Mom?"

Paula shrugs, "I don't know. I just don't know with the two of them. It might not be a good idea."

"I think it is if you still love her. She loves you and always has. And love's enough!" And then Maggie blushes and laughs.

I drink my tea and give her a look, of what I'm not sure. She's family, both funny and infuriating. No point reminding her of the ups and downs. Once she was old enough, she too had learned to take care of my depressions, those post-Kat-depressions.

Maggie pulls out her photo album and puts the picture of us in it. "Do you have the rest of them? You kept them, didn't you? I remember us collecting them all up for you when you built your home up there in the Ortiz."

"Yeah, there's still quite a few in my trunk. I'll get them out for you sometime. With all the postcards we sent each other! A trunkful!"

"You do? Let's look at them together. That'll be hilarious. We can show Katie and Mike when they come. Who else are we inviting? David and Jamie, obviously."

"Obviously."

"And Charlie and anyone he wants to bring. Is Samantha invited? Or Rian? Or Tom? I liked him, a good steady friend for you after all of that. He's still in Colorado, right? Anyone else you can think of?"

"I don't know how big to make this. I think I'd prefer just the close family with us. And make it fun. Does David still play in that band? Maybe we could get a few of them to come and play for us. I'd love to have a dance party."

"Are your knees up for it? I'm not sure mine are." Paula was never much for dancing at the best of times, so I laugh at her lame excuse, so to speak. She stands up and does a twirl, a sashay and then a little curtsy for us both before sitting back down, grimacing as she says that's the extent of it.

"David can get more firewood so we can have a big bonfire outside in the afternoon while the food's cooking. Oh, where are we doing this?"

We hadn't talked about that. Paula and I look at each other, unsure. I don't want it to be at my house but I can't ask.

"You don't want it at yours, do you?" she says. "I can tell. But you don't want to ask, either! Some things never change! Yes, we'll do it up on Goldmine at the family home. We can set up the studio and the guest cabins for everyone."

I grin. I can still do that part. With David and John's help, that is. I volunteer the three of us to clean them out and stock them with candles and firewood and drinking water. Maggie works out the chores we each need to take on. It's less than three weeks, closer to two.

"Do we tell them?"

"We can. It seems only fair. And that way, the scene is set and I won't be making a mess of it for anyone, right?"

"I still think you should invite Kat, or at least tell her."

I shake my head. "No. I can't and you can't, either. Promise?"

She promises but I don't fully trust her.

"So what exactly is the problem? Can anything be done for you, Joey?" She quickly comes back to the subject at hand.

"Yes and no. It's a malignant brain cancer. In someone younger, they'd probably do surgery. But for someone my age? It's not worth it. Just prolongs my life for a little while but I'd be in pain, anyway. Chemo isn't pretty for anyone. Dr. Nan went into detail about this kind of cancer; it starts with a word like globi, globular? I don't know. I didn't see the point in learning! It's a big word. A long one. Dr. Nan tells me that there are all these pain medications she can give me when the headaches get too bad, or when I just need to zone out."

"What headaches?"

"I've been having headaches, kinda like migraines in intensity. That and the falling over, that's what made her start checking me out. I don't have any family history to look into, so we're playing it by ear. I had these really bad headaches a few months ago. And I kept slipping and sitting down quickly. So I talked to her. She helped. Got some strong medicines. The headaches come and go now. Not too bad. I try not to drive, though, not much, anyway, the vertigo scares me. That's about it, really."

Paula shakes her head. "Not quite. Can I come with you next week to talk to her? See what we need to know? How to help?"

Maggie agrees and they talk together, about which one will drive us. They start organizing the next week for me. Part of me wants to tell them to leave it alone. I'm getting claustrophobic with this attention. Don't know how to take it. But I sit back and listen. I know that this is for them now, not about me. But for them. My family of choice. They want to take care of me the way they know how. I bet I'll get food in the fridge, too.

"Do you need more whiskey up there?"

That surprises me, that Maggie would offer to replenish my liquor, but why not! "Yeah, especially with all of you visiting me. I need some beer for David and his friends, too. We could go shopping together if you want."

Maggie laughs. "You're not that sick! I know you hate shopping. We'll do it, right, Mom? Give us a list and we'll pick up the party food on the same day. It'll be fun. I'll get John to come with us and carry the bags. He'll love that!" She giggles at the thought of woodsman John following them around Albertson's on a weekday afternoon.

. "Well, it's time to head back before the roads ice up—is that okay with you two?" Paula looks tired. We all stand up and clear away the plates and cups. In the kitchen I look for the car keys.

"Yeah, but I'm driving this time, Paula."

Maggie laughs out loud as she gets us our coats. "You two always fight about Mom's driving. Not that I'm saying anything about it."

Paula grabs the keys and races to the car.

Chapter Thirty

I make another fire. The snow has been with us for a week now. I'm not snowed in. Not exactly. But I don't want to drive. Not down the dirt road when I'm a little shaky to start with. The headaches have come back, with a new strength that wipes me out. I sleep a lot. Luckily, Fred doesn't need many walks these days. He's happiest next to the fire with me. I read. I've given up on the classics. I read my postcards, instead.

I'm making a scrapbook for Maggie. And it's fun. To relive all the shenanigans of my life. I read and sit and sip my whiskey. Abstinence be damned. I once saw a billboard with the advice: Abstinence is the choice of love. I wanted to add: Passion is the choice of lovers!

This morning, I opened up a whole new envelope of letters and cards from Spain, which was the first stop I made when I moved to Europe at forty-two. I'd traveled and lived there for three years, more or less. Maggie was the one I wrote to. And she was the one to tell Kat where to find me. Did I know that at the time? I wonder. I must have.

It was shortly after breaking down outside the local bar when Kat told me to leave her alone again. So much for any kind of sympathy. Which got me that stitch in my tongue. After that, I'd talked to a head-doctor in Santa Fe.

I knew I was on the edge again. I knew I'd hit some point where I couldn't talk to Kat, or even have any contact with her.

What to do? We lived in the same town. We saw each other around. What to do now that the affair had messed me up again? I kept to myself. I hardly even saw Paula. She hadn't wanted me to get involved. Probably because she could see the ending. This ending. The one where I'd lose myself.

So I stayed home. Maggie came over most days, with or without John. Chris, Mike and Charlie came over, Mike stayed and cooked with me and worked on the place. He preferred fixing up my cabin to working with his brother and dad. Fine by me. I had easy company. We became close. Not so shy with each other. He talked of wanting to join the army. His parents were completely horrified by the idea. I figured it was his life. So I listened. That alone got me out of my head.

I went to the doctor three times a week to start with. I drove through the north side of Back Road to get home and I avoided Kat's end of town. I'd heard she had a huge opening, inviting everyone from around here. I didn't go. Maggie did. She told me that Kat looked stunning, and also that it seemed she and Mark were fighting—he was all grumpy, even at the party. Maggie told me I should go, show my face, and that Kat would fall in love with me all over again.

But I didn't want to fall in love. I couldn't take any more.

Chapter Thirty-One

I flew to Madrid, Spain in March, 1982. I stepped off the plane and smiled so widely the other passengers teased me in Spanish for my obvious appreciation. I found a bus that took me into town. I walked around with the backpack slung over my shoulders and notebook in hand. I wanted to walk and listen and absorb as much as any desert sponge in a flash flood. I sat at a café on the side of a plaza. Thick black coffee with a local liquor to follow. I watched. I breathed in. I relaxed.

I'd escaped. I'd escaped Kat.

A Chicago magazine had asked me to write about the shifting economics in Spain, now that it was joining the European Economic Community. A time of great unemployment, massive inflation and high public spending on outdated state institutions. The leftovers from Franco and thirty years of fascism and communism. The country was in huge upheaval, trying for democracy while suffering economically.

Flights to be paid for, some basic living expenses, and numerous articles upon publication. Potentially a book contract with a national publishing house. That was enough for me. At forty-something, I was about to start over once again.

Dr. Wills agreed. A change of scene would help me move on. Take charge of my life again. Living less of it in reaction to Kat and this repetitive affair of ours.

That afternoon, as I sat at the café bar, I wrote to Maggie and Paula and everyone to let them know I was safe and sound and not to worry. Luckily, before I'd left, Mike had agreed to stay in my house for the six months I planned on being in Spain. With Jimmy and Angel, the dogs, the plants, the truck, all his, he'd have a home to call his own at twenty. Not bad for the kid. And it kept him out of the armed forces. Sneaky of me, but it worked for all of us. Paula had given me a huge thankful hug when I'd told her my plan.

I sat on the square until the sun sank and the chill hit me. Nothing like a winter in New Mexico, but still, it was time to find a pension. My Spanish came back to me quickly, and I asked the waiter where he recommended. He pointed me up the road and to the left. Friends of his had a five-room hostel. Close by and cheap, he told me. Perfect.

I paid up and set out to find a room. The streets seemed narrow, full of the remnants of a market, bits and pieces of fruit and vegetables scattered along the edges. I walked past bags of trash and beautiful tall old brick buildings, older than any I'd ever seen before in my own country. I walked with my head turning every few seconds, up and down, staring through shutters and into stores, homes and kitchens. And still I kept grinning. I couldn't help it.

This was just what the doctor ordered, literally!

I woke up to a commotion at some unheard-of early hour. I looked at my watch, the Russian pocket watch I rarely was without. Ah, right, local time, noon. Not so early then. My body denied the truth of that and claimed it was still five am. I snuck a look out the shutters and found myself looking down on stalls with colored plastic toys, clothes piled deep across wooden tables, and all the noise and chaos of a thriving market. Incredible.

I smelled coffee and something sweet. That got me dressed.

Down in the lobby, I greeted the caretakers, and we chatted for a while before I could go find my much-needed coffee. On my way to the café I'd been to, I saw a cart with donut-like strips being dunked in hot oil. Smelled so good that I stopped and asked what they were called.

"You never had churros?" the young dark-haired woman asked me in surprise.

I told her that I'd had one night in her country so far. She smiled as she pulled out two churros from the still hot oil, then covered them in white sugar and wrapped them in a paper cone for me. She wouldn't take any money, telling me that she knew she'd see me every day from now on! I took a bite. Incredible. Perfect. She handed me a cup of hot chocolate, so thick that the liquid barely dripped when I dunked my churro in it. I thanked her and then we talked a while as I sat at the table beside her. She told me how they make them a little differently in each part of Spain. That then could be my first homework. Researching donuts.

Full and happy, I walked back to the plaza I'd seen the day before. I nodded at the waiter at the café and sat down. I looked around at all the activity. Holiday feeling. The water fountain had kids playing in it.

The streets were decorated in streamers and garlands, and flowers lined the shop fronts. Semana Santa, I was told, the Easter celebrations of this Catholic country, were about to kick in with parades, bonfires and live music for the next week. This was a perfect time to come to a new country, during its greatest festival! Everyone was celebrating, playing music in the streets, the children were out of school, and the knowledge of the unbelievable numbers of unemployed couldn't dampen the spirits here.

I chatted and wrote and walked the city as much as possible, discovering ancient cathedrals, medieval monuments, fountains everywhere, and every day I stumbled across markets that attracted people from all over the country.

I thrived. I loved it.

After two months, I decided to head north. I hitched up the one main road, not much by American standards, still one lane most of the way, packed with trucks crossing into France. I sat with a driver from Bilboa.

Miguel was Basque. A separate country, as far as he was concerned. I realized that this was a little known topic in the U.S., how the countries are divided up over in Europe, the culture and economics of each one a rich story of its own. I listened as he talked of the ETA, the Basque freedom fighters, how the locals respected and helped them undermine the Spanish government. I heard of old-school terrorism and was reminded of the Mayan guerrillas in Guatemala. I knew I would find out more. And I did.

I stayed with his family for a week. We drank too much. They played music all night long and then woke early to work at the steel factories. The Basque country was doing better than most, probably due to rich minerals and easy access to export goods to the rest of Europe.

I laughed with Miguel over his wife's teasing him for his weight, for sitting in a truck all day long while she carried and lifted huge boxes at the factory down the road.

"And you, Joey. Too skinny. We need to get you a good local girl to marry. How old did you say you were?" She picked at the loose shirt tucked into my jeans. "You need fattening up. Come, let's cook you some more fritters and omelets and less of those salads you crave. More garlic fried in olive oil! And wine. You don't drink enough, Joey. You need to fatten up!" They all laughed with her, and decided to try to fix me up.

I wasn't ready for that, so I'd ended up leaving for Santander, a city only a few hours away on the northern coast. I took a bus and found a campsite outside of town, which was high above a beach, Matalenas, which you reached by climbing down two hundred steps carved into the cliffs.

I swam. I talked to the bartender. He told me about the tourists and how the great weather there kept his income steady despite everything. I supported his business most days. For selfless reasons.

Chapter Thirty-Two

My first class was a disaster.

I'd signed up to teach English in Valencia,. I spoke the language, right? Couldn't be that bad, right?

"Hello. My name is Joey. I'm from New Mexico. And I'm here to help you learn English. Who can do what? Do you know about the past tense yet? Or the future? Not that the future is all that it's cut out to be!"

Nothing. No one spoke. They looked at me in a stunned silence. I tried explaining again. Where I was from and asking what they needed from me. Ah, shit. Nothing. Back to basics. I tried not to use Spanish to translate, which was a big no-no, I'd been told.

"Me, Joey." And I pointed to myself.

"Me, Joey." They repeated.

"No, no. Your name is?"

"No, no. Your name is?" they repeated.

The hour killed me. It didn't get any easier. Afterwards, though, one of the students came up to me and introduced herself in English.

"My name is Rian. How are you, Joey? Did you like teaching us?"

And she laughed at the expression on my face. And then she switched to Spanish, explaining she knew the basics but wanted to watch this charming teacher make a total mess of it. "I have some English grammar books if you want to borrow them. It'll help you."

I shook her hand. "Yeah, I think I need help. Want to be my assistant? I'll need one if today is anything to go by."

"Have you ever taught before?" Rian stood in front of me, smiling softly, grinning at my discomfort. Was she flirting with me or is this normal to have a young beautiful female student touching your arm after class?

I stuttered. "No, well, I taught my friends' kids to read a long time ago. I didn't know what I was doing, luckily they were smart enough to figure it out!"

"Come on, then. Let's go back to my place and get you some books. You have some homework to do before class tomorrow." And she headed down the steps of the school and across the yard with me following, finally finding my words, and asking about her life here. A schoolteacher. From up near Madrid, but working the academic year in Valencia, where the work was. Her village was suffering too badly in the latest inflation's chaos. No work there. So here she was.

I walked at her side, and we laughed over my first attempt at teaching formally. She stood as tall as me; slender build with curves in the right place, long hair tied back, and dark brown eyes that sparkled when she smiled. She smiled a lot. She practically skipped down across the park to her apartment in the old neighborhood.

Long winding cobble streets led us to an old hotel, recently split into separate apartments. Up two flights and she unlocked her door, inviting me in. She threw her bags on the table and found a bottle of red wine for us in the kitchen. I looked out her windows onto the ocean in the distance. She came and passed me a glass.

"To teachers! May we all enjoy each day and all of our students!" and we clinked glasses. I spent the rest of the evening with her, and enjoyed her easy light spirit. Laughing at herself and her life in the city, she told me about her village in the desert. I told her of Madrid, New Mexico, and all about my home there, the dogs, and the landscape, and then about my friends.

"So why leave?"

"I needed a break from this relationship that was driving me crazy. Long story. Don't worry about it! I'm here and happy to be here. And you? Are you dating anyone?"

"Not right now. My parents think I should be married by now."

"Why?"

"I'm thirty-two, and that's old for a good Catholic girl. But they like that I'm a teacher and I send them money each month. So it is all right for them, but they would like grandchildren some day. I don't want any, though. Too many children in the world without homes."

We talked about growing up in small towns, and the way our lives have brought us here. Yes, we flirted. But I left. After four hours with Rian, I left and walked home. Smiling to myself as I walked. Only half a mile away, I came to my own small apartment overlooking the Mediterranean Sea.

The next morning, I knocked on her door.

"Who is it?"

"Joey, the English teacher." I answered, stuttering slightly. I wasn't sure I should've come back so early, but I'd spent the night dreaming about Rian, and had woken in such a bright mood, I wanted to share it with her. I waited. She opened the door in an old green dressing gown. Her hair was down. She looked gorgeous. I grinned. "I forgot to take those grammar books!"

"I was wondering if you'd think about that. Come on in. Make us some coffee. I'm going back to bed."

And she did. And so did I.

I brought her coffee in bed for months after that. Even if I hadn't stayed the night with her, I'd come over in the mornings and wake her with fresh ground coffee and churros, if I could find them.

What a beautiful way to spend three years in Valencia; with Rian at my side. While living in Spain, I became a writer. For real. I wrote for American magazines, ones in England and, after my Spanish recovered, I wrote for the Madrid newspapers. The observations of a foreigner, an ex-patriot, looking at the political and economic upheavals in their own country, and they loved it all. I still tried to teach part-time, but I never really got the hang of it. In fact, Rian ended up co-teaching with me most of the time, which the other students thought was hilarious. They constantly teased us, but we never minded. In fact, it added a spice to the silliness we shared.

Anyway, I wrote. I studied the Spanish culture, the artists and the writers. I became fascinated by the artwork of Salvador Dali. The year I'd arrived, the stories in the papers told of his senile wife poisoning him, to the point where his nervous system fell apart and his hands shook uncontrollably. The king was an unofficial admirer until the last few years of Dali's life. The last drawing of Dali's ended up being of the King. A mutual fan club.

I had read so much about these artists and writers, Federico Garcia Lorca, Joan Miro, and others, that I felt part of their world. I was no creative genius like them, but I knew I had to write in order to make sense of my world. I understood. They inspired me. And I needed that sense of belonging to something greater than myself. And so I wrote as much as I could, waking at six in the morning, spending an hour with pen on paper before waking Rian. In bed.

One summer, she took me up to her hometown of Toledo, just southeast of Madrid, a high desert town. Small enough to walk to the outskirts, yet enough anonymity that I could enter a bar, have a drink and write undisturbed.

The train from Valencia took all morning. And by lunchtime, we pulled into this deserted station. No one greeted the train, and the waiting rooms were empty. I followed Rian through the exit gates. She pulled me down the main road toward the plaza.

"I want to show you something," she said as we ran and skipped in the midday sun. The gravel road took us past the supermarket, closed, the bars, closed, and the schools, all closed. Siesta time. The town was dead. We ran, the two of us, through the sleepy streets until she stopped and pointed. In the middle of the plaza was the most glorious fountain I had ever seen. Tall, imposing, with water that flowed, splashed and cascaded on and on; the sound filled my ears and I could hardly hear her.

"Come!" and Rian drew me closer. She climbed into the pond underneath the waterfall, fully dressed. I couldn't resist. I followed her. We stood there, laughing, soaked and silly. "This was my favorite place to be as a kid. Mom would come find me here every day! She'd scold me, but I think that she wished she could join me in here!"

We'd walked to her parents' home, all closed up and with shutters pulled shut, protecting the home from the intense heat. Her mother opened the door to two drowned wanderers, and luckily for me, she pulled us inside, laughing and hugging us both. She started chatting away as she gave us towels and dry clothes. Rian and I were given separate rooms. Catholic girls in their thirties are still virgins for their parents. We played along and they adored me.

The family always treated me sweetly each month, when we came to visit. Even when Rian told them that I'd be leaving her. For the U.S. For Kat. The decision had been almost impossible to make.

Chapter Thirty-Three

Rian and I took a trip to Madrid, to work our way through El Rastro, the huge flea market, one Sunday morning. We'd wanted new clothes for ourselves, and books for the kids at her school. We split up, planning to find each other at the bar on the plaza near La Latina metro station. I was wandering aimlessly along the Calle de Ribera de Curtidores, checking out the side streets with their stalls full of used clothes. My brain switched off. I daydreamed. Shopping has never been a strong point of mine. I walked. I touched stuff. I bought nothing. I looked around and watched other foreigners shopping and haggling and buying armloads. I saw Kat.

I stood still. I stared. I watched her buy a stripy red and blue shirt from a gypsy and her kids. I stood stockstill as people walked around me, pushing me impatiently. I stared. Kat turned in my direction.

I ran.

As fast as I could in those crowded streets, I ran. Back to Rian. Back to the bar, to the plaza, to the station. I hid inside the bar, in the far corner. I talked to the waiter and described Rian to him, asking him to watch out for me, so that I wouldn't miss her. I hid in the back. I drank red wine. More than enough. I sat at the wooden table, on my own.

And when Rian found me there three hours later, I told her all about Kat. Finally, I told her why I had left the U.S., my home and animals and friends in the mountains. Rian listened and she understood. She kissed me sweetly and said, Let's go home. And so we caught the next bus south.

Now she knew. And still she loved me.

Chapter Thirty-Four

I pull out the Russian hat, my dad's hat from so long ago. I can't picture him any longer. Not really. I think of him as tall and redheaded. The height might be because I was still so young. And short. The red hair is a hand-me-down I live with, even now. Especially down there, in my nether regions, where I'm still quite red! You probably didn't need to know that, right?

What else is here? More photos. More letters. Some of the sweetest love letters from Kat, about why she adored me, the sensuality we shared, the creative challenge of living up to each other's ideals, the raw passion that deepened every time we were together. The words are lyrical, poetic yet grounded in detail. Too personal to read right now. It might weaken my resolve to keep my distance from her. In my heart, I hope she'll come back, but what if she didn't? If this wasn't enough to bring her back to me for one last time? How horrendous would that be? I can't risk it. I'd prefer not to find out that her love was unable to deal with that level of intensity. That my death was inconvenient for her. What a devastating thought. Nope, I prefer not to find out.

I pull out her boots. Typical, eh? I'm trying not to think about her too much, and here she is again. The boots smell like her still. How old are they now? Some thirty years? How funny to think I'd kept them so long. She was going to throw them out one spring, or was it the winter I'd come back from Spain?

I remember the night, though. I saw her put them in the trash can. I'd been watching her place for a few hours, wondering whether to knock or not. I saw her throw them out. I watched her go back into the gallery-home of hers. No sign of Mark. No sign of any new lover. Then she came out and climbed into the Land Rover and drove off. I walked up to the trashcan and stole them. I hid them in my coat and walked home quickly. I put them next to the sculpture of her, next to my bed in the loft she knew so well.

Mike had moved out and into the family home next door for a few months while I worked for his dad again. I needed solo time. I could've lived with him, but I think I needed to be alone. He understood. He packed up his things. He did seem different toward me, more belligerent, but I put it down to his age. I should've asked. I didn't. I wish I had.

I've kept other things of Kat's, as well. I have her favorite book. A book of poems from her own grandmother, from when she first came to America. There is a sketch of her dad she'd made as a kid. And I love this photo of us in the Jemez. At the springs, naked in the snow, I'd held the camera for us. Beautiful smiles from the both of us. Another magical day out together.

Do I tell too much of the harsh stuff? I might. We did have magical times together, but the darkness overshadows many of those memories. I wish it weren't so, but it is. The words of love, desire and deep intimate knowing are lost in the agony of my breakdowns.

Here is a scarf of Rian's. From when I left her at the airport that last time we saw each other. She was wrapped up warm against the winter winds of Madrid. I held her close. She tore the scarf off and wrapped it round my neck, tucking it in securely.

"Take care of your heart, Joey." And that was all she said before kissing me goodbye and walking away, not looking back. Bittersweet tenderness has always been my undoing.

On the plane, I curled up and stared out the window, wondering why on earth I would leave someone so good as she was. I never got an answer.

The scarf is kind of musty today, but maybe I'll wear it for this winter. I take it out and lay it on the corduroy armchair. One of the cats comes over and claims it. Perfect.

I find a photo of my father from in the '40s. He'd come back from Europe, the war and there he is in his uniform, with his arms around my mother and me, aged five. Young and scared—that's not what you expect, is it? I'm supposed to look happy to see him. I think the photo tells it all. We didn't like him.

There is a great one of my mom, petite, dark-haired, dress flying and both of us laughing with me in her arms, as she's swinging me around and around in the summer's evening sky.

David knocks on the door and lets himself in, calling out as he does that he has more groceries from his mom, and some beer for us to drink together. He shakes himself and takes his boots off, then sets the paper bag down next to the kitchen table.

"Still thinking of using all four chairs, Joey?" he teases me.

"Well, yeah, actually I am! We're having a Thanksgiving party."

"Mom told me. We've got people coming next week. At her house, though, right?"

David sits down next to me by the trunk and passes me an open beer. He tips one in a salute. "Cheers!"

I can't *not* tell him. I take a sip and give him my news and the reasons we decided to pull everyone together this month.

"Wow. Shit. I don't, I don't know what to say, Joey."

He leans forward in his chair and stares into his beer. It's quiet for ten minutes or so and then he turns to me asking who the hell can he talk to when I'm gone? He shakes his head. He drinks more beer. And then he apologizes quietly for thinking only about himself. We both finish our beers in silence. I figure he needs time before we talk more. I wait. He sits back. And looks at me. "What do you need?"

"Oh, David, I need us to hang out and talk and drink beer. And not to change these afternoons of ours over the next few months."

"And the animals?" He scratches Kit-Kit's ears and looks over at Fred and the other cat napping on the bed together.

"I haven't worked that out."

"Well, they come with me then, okay? I love them all. I don't want them to lose each other, too. That would be mean." David's voice is loud. Strident. He needs this, I see

"Thanks. I'd love that." And then I have to look away. It's too much for me. I try my beer but it's still empty. I go and get us another. I pause at my window. It's getting dark already. Days are going too quickly for me.

I open the bottles and come give one to David. He's looking at Kat's boots. "When did you get her boots? That's kind of weird."

"Now, now! I've had them a long time. Remember how she always wore them? All months of the year, there she was in big boots. That's the weird part."

David laughed. "True. Is she coming for Thanksgiving?"

"I wish you hadn't asked. Everyone asks me that. I don't think so. I can't tell her. But you're bringing Jamie, right? I'd like to meet her."

"Yes, we're coming together. She loves the idea of meeting you all, the big wonderful crazy family of mine. I'm not so sure." David smiles anyway, and I know he's happy to have her with him. Good. I hope he has an easy love life. I don't know how to do that myself, but I want my friends to relax and love gently, whatever that means.

"What's this?" and David reaches into the trunk. He pulls out a stein from Oktoberfest in Munich.

I laugh. "Ah, yes, more trouble! I'd hitched across Germany with a friend of mine, this English guy in his twenties. I was forty-eight or something. We were both living in Freiberg, near France, and we'd woken up one morning with a killer hangover. He wanted some beer and I thought, 'Why not! Let's get to the Oktoberfest in Munich!'

It took us all day, some four hundred miles, and most drivers weren't too crazy about me being so old—they thought I must be a complete loser to hitchhike! We had a crazy time getting there and it just continued for two days. I'd only been over there for a few weeks when we did that. Such adventures I had in Europe, no wonder I kept going back." I stare out the window.

David brings me back with a question. "What happened then?"

"Steve got us to take a train home, but we took the wrong one and woke up at six am in Switzerland. Not quite where we thought. And the ticket man wasn't too willing to let us get back to Freiberg for free. But Steve was a real charmer and he sweet-talked us into getting home again. Not the last time I've been thrown off a train, but one of the funniest! Steve was short, a fiery Londoner with a strong Cockney-like accent, even when talking in German. I wonder what happened to him?"

David gets up and takes out some chips from the grocery bag. He offers me some. "When else were you thrown off a train? I can't say it's ever happened to me, not yet, anyway."

I get a postcard from the trunk. "Remember how I went to Spain with Kat earlier that summer? She'd come to travel with me; I'd invited her this time. Anyway, we decided to explore as much as we could by train. We ran out of money in Gibraltar. I wrote to your grandma to bail me out. See?" and I handed him a card of the Rock of Gibraltar from the late '80s. I'd scribbled that we were stuck in the south and I needed to get home to work in Germany. Could she help? Apparently not! I didn't hear back from her.

So we'd jumped onto a train heading to Madrid. Thrown off just south. In Toledo, of all places."

"And, let me guess, you went to your ex-girlfriends house?" David laughs and eats chips.

I grin, and shrug kind of embarrassed, because he was right, it had seemed the right thing to do. At the time. We spend the next four hours talking about Europe and how he'd love to go sometime. I pick a map off the shelves and hand it over. Kind of old, I tell him, but it'll be fascinating to take with you when you go, to see how the countries themselves have changed since then, the borders and the names even.

"Really?"

I nod and open it up on the floor and we both start making dream trips up as we chat. I'd love to help him travel there. I wonder how? More stories, if nothing else—I can inspire him with my own adventures and maybe he'll feel like he can do it, too. Who gave me the courage? My dad? In some strange way, I think it was Dad. His craziness. His determination to do what he wanted when he wanted. He inspired me. He fed me stories of other worlds. And I followed in his footsteps.

"Where's my hat?" I stand up and walk toward the trunk. "I can't see it."

"It's right there," says David. "On the left."

I can't see it. I can't see. Red and orange lights pulsate, blocking everything else. I try talking to David, telling him that I can't see it. Getting impatient. Rude. No shapes. Nothing real. No hat. Where's the damn hat? I just had? I fumble. I stumble. I can't see anything but for those hot colors. I crumble to my knees, asking for the hat.

"I can't see. David." My voice shakes. "I think I need a doctor."

And I black out. Gone.

Chapter Thirty-Five

I wake up screaming.

"It's all right, Joey. We're here." Maggie murmurs to me these words over and over. I hear David shout out of the door that they needed a doctor. He comes back and puts my hand in his. It is strong, reassuring. I squeeze back. I stop screaming.

I can't see. I can't see.

No one speaks.

Maggie caresses my wrinkled face, wiping away my tears. She puts my hand in hers and

I feel her own tears, instead. We say nothing. Too terrified.

I'm in the hospital, contained by hospital sheets, smelling the hospitals' disinfectants. I hear heavy steps come our way. A door opens and in walks someone officious, determined. I cringe. The warm voice surprises me.

"Hello, Joey. I'm Dr. Cooper. You're going to be okay. This isn't permanent. You had an episode that took us by surprise, that's all. The headaches came back, or so your doctor tells me. How badly?"

"Strong, but I had those pills for them. I was doing okay."

Dr. Cooper sits down on the bed. He reaches over and removes a bandage from my eyes, explaining as he goes that this can happen with brain tumors. Unpredictable. But he's not worried that this means we need to panic yet.

Maggie laughs derisively. "How can we not panic when Joey blacks out like that? It's terrifying! What are we supposed to do? What was David supposed to do?"

I turn my head to where David had held my hand. "David? Are you there?"

Faintly, I hear him hold back a cry, but he answers yes in a shaky voice. "I'm here."

"Are you okay? I'm so sorry, David. That was too quick. Too much in one afternoon. I'm so sorry." He reaches and holds me again, and squeezes me hard. We say nothing more. The doctor waits a moment.

"Okay, Joey, I need you to open your eyes slowly. It's pretty dark in here, right now. So it won't hurt. So, take your time, and open your eyes, okay?"

"Okay."

I breathe in. I breathe out. I open my eyes. Golden colors greet me. I blink, over and over. The doctor suggests he turn on a light in the corner and he gets up off the bed. I rub my eyes like a sleepy kid. I start making out shapes. I sense Maggie to my right. David to my left. And the doctor. I can see the doctor. I smile at him. And then Maggie starts crying in earnest. David runs to his mom and hugs her, smothering her against him.

I cry in relief. "I can see."

"Describe it for me."

"Fuzzy, but I can see you all. Bright but not the scary colors flashing at me like before."

"Good. I think we'll keep you in overnight. I want to watch your vitals. And maybe take an MRI in the morning to see how it's going inside you. I can't send you home. You live alone, right?"

David pipes up that he lives half a mile away, and that he is my nearest neighbor. Dr. Connor says I'll need help. That I can't live alone. In case this happens again, which it might. And that is exactly what I dread, having hospice care, or getting stuck in a hospital, not being home with my beloved animals, sitting on the porch, watching for David to drive by. I can't stay in here. I start to get out of bed with tubes hanging off me, the gown falling off my bare backside. Who cares what I look like, I can't stay. I'm shouting in panic.

The doctor tries to hold me down. I push him off. I'm no wimp! I climb out the other side of the bed, aiming for the door, and end up standing in front of Maggie. She stares at me. Her face is drained, pale and tear-streaked, her make-up smudged. "Get in bed. Now." And there is no messing with her.

"We'll take care of this, Joey. You stay tonight. I'll be here with you. Tomorrow you come home. Even if I have to move in myself, you are going home." And she starts crying again, trying desperately to stay brave but failing miserably. I can hardly see her through my own hopeless rage and tears.

David comes and helps me back in bed. He nods. "Don't think we'll leave you here alone."

Dr. Cooper suggests we have a few moments to get back to an even keel, and then he'll be back to talk about what to expect in the next stages, and all that he needs for us to decide.

I come home but it feels different. No longer truly mine. David has moved in. His jacket is hanging by the front door, with a pair of work boots underneath. He calls out to me from outside, near the back shed. He walks up to us with a huge smile. "I know how much you hate company, Joey. So I came up with a great plan! Want to hear?"

Maggie leads me to the woodstove to warm up after a cold ride home in her old Honda. I'm a little shaky. It's been a long three days. Too many tests for my liking. Maggie was a trooper, standing next to me all the way. John brought us both clean clothes and snuck in some chocolate and a beer for me! Good man. Paula cooked me healthy food from her greenhouse, and sat with me for hours on end, sometimes chatting, mostly quiet.

I sit down in my favorite armchair and immediately the critters head my way. I scratch and pet and rub each of them, then sit back with a sigh as they all claim their places on top of my lap and at my feet. David brings Maggie and me fresh coffee. He offers us cookies that he'd made in the solar oven the day before. Pretty good oatmeal cookies. I eat three.

"Okay, so ready for my ideas? I know we told Dr. Cooper that I'd move in to the studio room, but I don't know if you want me here all the time. So Dad and I fixed up our camper and brought it over. I parked it behind the sheds, out of sight. I put in walkie-talkies for us. Channel nine. Anyway, I'm here. Kind of. And you get your home to yourself, but for our coffee in the mornings and beer talk in the evenings." He rushes out the last sentence. Excited. Happy with his solutions.

It's more than I'd like, more company, but I'm too tired. I no longer know what's reasonable. Between the doctor and all that he told me, I'm shaken. My plans for a quiet, gentle decline at home seem to be unattainable. I want to sleep in my own bed. I want to die in my own bed.

Maybe this is the way to go. To be with David. But for him? Can I ask him to do this? I look at his mom questioningly. She nods, reading me so easily. David is waiting for me. "Thanks, kid. That sounds like a plan. I can do that. Can you?"

He grins again and nods.

"All right, then. What else has changed around here?" I look between them both.

Maggie leans back in her chair, thankful that I'm not going to get belligerent on her only child. She drinks her coffee and passes me the cookies before taking another herself. "Mom is on her way over. She wanted to pick up some things for you on the way, not sure what. Flowers, knowing her, and some herbal concoctions for you."

"Pot!" adds David with a smile.

Maggie gives us both a disapproving look. "I hope not. You know what I think about that habit of yours! Anyway, Mom and I called nearly everyone, and all but Rian can make it. She said she's going to write to you and send it off this week. She sends big love to you, and wanted you to know she loves the books you've sent her. She's enjoying Toledo and Madrid both these days, but it's too cold for her tastes. We had a great chat. I can tell you more at another time. Who else? Mike and Katie are getting here a couple of days before the party. Oh, that's soon! I wonder if they'll rent a car in Albuquerque?"

"Probably. You know he doesn't like being dependent on us, right?"

Maggie smiles sadly. "No, he doesn't like to ask for much. I wonder who taught him that, Joey?"

David laughs in delight; he loves it when his mom teases me.

Maggie continues. "Sam is coming, with the two grandkids! Can you imagine! All of them. She said Tom is working on getting a ride down here in the next day, too. Samantha's family is staying at the B&B in Madrid. Tom is coming to stay at my house in town, easier on him since he's not so good on his feet. Charlie is bringing a friend with him on Wednesday. It'll be a full house! I can't wait, to be honest. Mike and Katie are staying at your place, right, David? Did that work out?"

David explains to me how it's perfect for all of them, as he gets his uncle to keep an eye on his place while staying in the camper over here. You see, there's been a couple of local kids squatting empty places around Madrid the last few months, moving on when they'd sold all they could. Not a pretty situation for anyone involved. It works out for Mike as it makes the whole trip less pricy, and they might stay longer if they want. And since Mike is bringing his girlfriend to a half-finished home nearby, maybe he'll want to help with the plumbing projects with David.

No one mentions telling Kat. I'm glad. I can't face her like this.

David takes his mom out to the camper and they leave me alone. The trunk is still lying open. I see Dad's black hat and I put it on. I grab Rian's scarf from under one of the cats and wrap myself with that, too. I look at Kat's boots but that would be going too far. I lean back in the chair.

I open the scrapbook. I'm running out of time. I know it now. I feel it. I want to finish this book for her. In the evenings, I'll work on it. When David is here, we can make food together, and I'll go through the last few piles of photos and letters from Europe.

The cats sleep on my lap. The fire warms me. Deeply.

I doze.

Chapter Thirty-Six

Eleanor comes to me in my dreams.

I think of those days in Wales together, when I was beginning to walk again, taking small hikes through the rainy afternoons, glad to be able to use my legs again. We bumped into each other on the Downs, and then again at the hotel in Rhossili, the one with the incredible views of the bay below. I'd loved it in that place. I'd spend hours at a time simply staring off into the horizon, watching the oil rigs, seagulls and clouds in equal measure. Daydreaming. Writing. Drinking a beer or two. Questioning myself. Judging myself.

But then one day, Eleanor joined me at the picnic table. A storm was building out over the waves. I watched the clouds gathering strength. And then Eleanor sat down opposite me and introduced herself formally.

Eleanor was an inch or two shorter than me, an outdoor woman, with a tan to show for it. We were both in our early fifties at that point. My hair was still long and tied back in a braid to my shoulders. She had a crew cut, and the color of her hair almost matched the steel blue-grey eyes that paid attention to me when I spoke. She wore sensible boots and a long, flowing green skirt. The simple, straightforward style complemented her striking good looks.

She flattered me with her questions. I asked her to join me for dinner.

We'd sat outside to start with, shared some scampi and chips, and then a few beers. I tried the local ale but it was too strong for me. She drank the darkest beer that wasn't quite a Guinness. I asked her about the area, as it was all pretty new and different to me. I'd only been there a year by then.

Southwest Wales, the Gower Coast, specifically, held close family ties for her. Generations of the Thomas clan came from, and inevitably returned to, Wales, or so I learned. The Thomases of Oxfordshire were farmers, with the inclination to visit other farmers on holidays. A busman's holiday like in the Second World War. She was no farmer, herself, but a teacher. At a University college in North London. Her husband had died a few years before. Her children were grown and out on their own. She was traveling alone. As was I.

In my early fifties, I'd needed to get out of Madrid, New Mexico again, and a new book project came to fruition. So since turning fifty-two, I'd been living in a small cottage just outside of a fishing village near Port Einon, Wales. I'd needed to write in peace. And the Gower offered a mix of small towns, farming land, uninhabited wild moors, open hills and huge dark dramatic coastlines. I loved it all. I was hooked.

"Tell me about your book," she said when we got the food in front of us.

"Only if you tell me about London!"

"Deal, but you go first."

I'd talked about how it all began for me, in Guatemala, this fascination of mine with how small communities farm as one. I wanted to understand how people live and work together. My own history being so disjointed, I grew up apparently compelled to find some community to belong in. And how impulse brought me here, another small village, and this time I came with a focus on the mix of farming and tourism. After the years in Madrid, there was a certain logic to living here in the Gower coast.

"Looking out over the ocean is as refreshing to me as staring out over the New Mexican empty mesas," I explained. We both turned and silently enjoyed the sight of the waves coming in to reclaim the beach in front of us.

She described her North London apartment, near a small square in Islington, a place that held markets on the weekends, and how it felt living in a small village within a culturally rich city.

"I love the neighborhood, and I love being able to walk or cycle to the museums and galleries in the West End. I went to see *Madame Butterfly* recently, and walking back with my son through the deserted streets at midnight was magical! We had the streets to ourselves, window shopping and making up stories about the workers in the city. Such fun we had."

After that, she asked me about my scars, and about why I needed a walking stick. She questioned me all about moving far away from family and my own culture, and why I had chosen absence as a source of reprieve. I talked and she understood.

She mentioned her own long distance walks through the fells and the highlands of Scotland after Brian had passed on. She knew how to hike for days at any one time, just she and her Border collie, an aging girl by the name of Derby. She looked closely at me as she talked, moments of quiet, seeing me for who I am. She never needed more.

I wake when David comes back in alone.

"Mom's gone," he tells me. "I'm about to go see Jamie. Can I bring her soon to meet you? I'd like to cook us some chicken and potato soup if you're up for it."

"I'd like that. When are thinking?"

"I'll ask her, and see if she has any time off before Thursday. She works at one of the galleries in Madrid until about five. If we can come over, I can pick her up at the Shaft, grab a quick drink and head back here after that. Oh, and I brought in a few armfuls of wood." David carries on chatting while getting ready to go out. He starts to fuss over me, but upon seeing me stare coldly at him, he stops sheepishly. "You can tell you raised me, right?"

And that makes me laugh. "Oh, yeah. But then again, Maggie pretty much took care of me a number of times too, so this feels normal. Don't worry. I'll tell you when you piss me off."

"Well, having a brain tumor hasn't stopped you from swearing." And he waves goodbye, grabbing his jacket from the steel hook. The door closes softly behind him.

I putter in the kitchen for an hour or so, making a plate of cheddar cheese and crackers, and I pour a glass of Cabernet Sauvignon. The home is still mine. I can do this. I love seeing the paintings and photos on the walls around me. I smile. It's good to be home.

I lie on my bed, not because I'm tired. But because I can. I roll around. I fart. I laugh. I then sit in each of the four chairs at the wooden table. I look out each window. I see the snow, and how it melted off one roof but not the other. I see the path that David has made to the outhouse from his trailer. He's cut yet more wood for us. I think I'll like having him so close. As much as I love Maggie and Paula, I don't think their staying here would work for more than a week. Too much mothering for the likes of me. Smothering.

It occurs to me that for the Thanksgiving party, I could have someone stay here if they need. There is the studio out back. It has its own door and a woodstove, what more would they need? I wonder who I could have live here with me? I mean, stay with me. Tom is set up at Maggie's. Paula has Charlie, right? Or was that someone else?

I can't remember stuff from only a few hours ago, but hell, the past is banging away in my head, making me pay attention. So much for the past flying speedily by when you know you're dying. I'm getting every moment of love and laughter revisited at my own convenience. All the time. No commercial breaks. And since I'm thinking of all those friends of mine, I wonder if Tom will come up here. I'd love to spend some time for just the two of us, reminiscing. He'd always had great stories of the farming communities in Central America, and now he has the wolves. He's a strange man, with a heart full of the troubles of others.

I head back into the studio and tidy up, putting clean sheets on the bed. It is a small ten-by-ten foot room with one window that's facing west, a large metal desk and drawers stuffed with my notes. I must remember to burn them soon. I hide the dust bunnies under the rug next to the window. I check to make sure the lamp still works. I throw another blanket on the bed. The room is chilly. I haven't been in here for weeks now. No more writing at this desk. I put away some rough drafts. I have no more to say. Not for the papers, anyway.

The room is now officially ready.

Back at the kitchen table, I pull out the glue and tape. I grab another shoebox of goodies from the trunk. I open more wine. Time to play. Time to daydream, eh? Yep. I'm ready. Memories? Bring them on!

Then again, I don't know what's going to come to mind now that I said that. Oh, shit. I get up and make a hot tea, instead.

Chapter Thirty-Seven

We'd bumped into each other at the Mine Shaft. No surprise there, but it was unplanned. It had been a few months since Kat and I had last seen each other. That had been just after I got back from Russia. I'd come back from Germany, curious to see her, but I avoided finding her.

Anyway, we bumped into each other, and hung out at the bar, chatting and laughing with Becky, the bartender. My sweet old dog, Jimmy, was playing on the porch as he does. He was one of the few dogs still allowed in here, since he always behaved himself, and stuck close or waited outside, and who can resist a fourteen-year-old dog? Everyone loved my sweet Husky boy. He'd grown up here, first with me and then with Mike. I watched him for a while. It was so good to have canine company again. I'd missed him.

Becky poured a Guinness and ale for us. She showed us the *New Mexican* newspaper with the cartoons and horoscopes. Not my thing, but Kat read them, anyway. Pisces, that's me. Aries for her. I heard some words but I didn't pay attention. I watched her lips. I wanted to lean in and taste her again.

"What? Oh!" and she blushed and laughed at herself for noticing my gaze.

I shook my head and tried to refocus. "Are we going to dance tonight? It's been a while."

"Sure. Why not. But only one or two. I should get home."

"Why? Is William still around?"

"Yes. And you know he doesn't like us hanging out together."

"Jealous?"

She grinned, and then dragged me onto the dance floor in front of the band. The Southwest Blue Country Band. Like I've said before, country is not my style, but if it means Kat and I get to dance, then I'll take anything. I've always loved the touch of her melting against me, the way our bodies remember and move as one. Such an intoxicating feeling. Addictive.

The band took a break after three songs so we sat at the bar again. I asked about William in my usual charming manner. "How is the insecure prick?"

"Joey!"

"Well, how can you stand it? At every moment, he wants to know where you are, and not just because I'm around, but with everyone. You're no fun with him next to you, babying his fragile state. It's tense, uncomfortable for all of us. You know how it is! He wants to know your every movement. How boring is that?"

"You're just pissed because we had to hide from him."

I finished my second beer. "Too damn right, I am. Don't you get tired of this crap? Did you tell him how great it was to be with me again? Can't you tell him we want to see each other?"

"Presumptuous, aren't you?" and then she pulled me up to dance with her, the perfect distraction. When we sat down, I kicked back in, though.

"Kat! Please! Why do you keep on avoiding me? Being with me again? And you end up picking these jealous lovers to live with! It's driving me crazy."

"And you're not jealous? Hah!"

"Okay. I am. We both know it. And you know why. I'm always on the outside, looking at you living with whoever's the latest, and knowing I can't talk to you, see you, except like this, when it's convenient. When you're alone or your lover is out of town, you come to me in the middle of the night. I hate it!"

"But I like it, to be honest." She waited a moment and then asked me if this really did make me crazy.

"You should know by now. Of course it does, never knowing how you feel, what you want. Telling our friends that there's nothing going on, and then, well, you know the rest. Why can't you just be with me? I don't get it." And I looked up again. She had tears in her eyes, her jaw was tight, and she whispered, "It means too much."

"To me?"

"No, to me."

She ordered another round for us, but this time, she got us Maker's Mark. We drank them down fast, staring at each other.

Then her eyes lit up, and she grabbed my hand and took me into the bathrooms when no one was looking. And she pulled me inside.

Chapter Thirty-Eight

There's a knock on the door. I open it to find Tom with a friend of his standing there, both of them dressed in thick coats, woolen hats and big snow boots. The snow is barely falling. Tom is six foot, his bald tanned head covered with a fur-lined hunters' hat. His wide smile breaks across the craggy scarred face and he takes a bow for me. Ever the show-off.

"My dear man! You look divine for these weary travelers!"

"Prepared for the worst then, are you?" I ask. And I step aside for them both.

Tom comes in and introduces Martin, a buddy from Colorado who was passing through to Southern New Mexico.

"I thought I'd come see if you want to join us for a burger and beer at the bar. It's still open, right, Joey?"

I close the door behind them. "What? Now?"

They both nod and grin. Tom assesses my home and gives his approval. "Yep, this is pretty similar to Guatemala. No wonder you liked the lifestyle there. You do realize it takes a lot to get me out of my home. I guess I still like you, after all!" and he hugs me tightly. "Good to see you, Joey. Let's go catch up, shall we?"

Martin explains that he's on his way to Las Cruces for the holiday week, so needs to eat and then drive some more today. He has about an hour or so before he drops off Tom at Maggie's. Sounds perfect to me. It's been quiet at home. David was working in Taos for the last two days. I had the place to myself, which I liked. But I got lost in the past. I needed to talk to someone in real time, if you know what I mean. I haven't left the house since getting out of hospital. This will be good practice for the party in a few days. Start talking to people again, and not just the critters.

The road is bare of snow because of the traffic, but there are some drifts starting to pile up on the sides. I stare out of the window and enjoy being a passenger, for once. They chat about the drive down through the pass at the border, but I hardly listen. I'm watching the clouds. I see a coyote stare at me as we pass. I smile at it and give thanks for another day.

The Mine Shaft Tavern changed hands fairly recently and the locals are still adjusting. We'd been used to a more lax attitude. They are trying to make money from the place, odd concept, I know, but it means new paint, and a sanded and oiled wooden floor, and higher prices. The main room is huge and they say it's the longest bar in the country. I never fully trust those claims. Who looked into it? It's an old school Western bar with honest live cowboys, hardcore biker gangs, back-to-the-landers and a bunch of dykes. It's quite a place. Not for the faint-hearted.

Once we arrive there, we are shown to the corner table near the fireplace, my favorite place during winter months. I introduce Timothy, the best waiter in the place. Timothy is in his early forties, full of energy with a new daughter and a beautiful wife who reminds me of Eleanor.

"Did you ever meet her?" I ask him.

Martin and Tom look at me worriedly.

"Oh, did you ask me something? Sorry, Timothy—I was thinking about your wife. She's like Eleanor was, something about her, I'm not sure what exactly. We lived up at the home I'm in now. I made it for her. For Eleanor, that is."

Timothy recovers the quickest; he's used to my wandering thoughts. "Yes, I remember her. You brought the family and me up when the boys were first born, didn't you? You showed me how you'd done the plastering inside since I was about to finish our place that summer. I'm sorry she passed on. Two years ago, was it?"

Timothy tells the others that we'd chatted for hours about building straw bale homes, and how impressed he was that a sixty-year-old could throw the bales around like I did! We'd become fast friends. Flattery does that.

"Hey, what are you all doing on Thanksgiving?" I ask him.

"We're coming here in the afternoon. The locals' dinner. Are you coming?"

"Not this time. Maybe I can drop by, though. I'm going up to Paula's and we're having a party with some old friends. A going-away party. It'll last all evening, knowing this lot! I'd love to have you come over. Want to bring the family? There will be other kids around for the boys to play with. Tom's sister is bringing her grandkids from Arizona."

Timothy takes directions. And then, he takes our order.

After he's gone to get the three pale ales, Tom turns to me. "Are you going to tell him?"

I shake my head. "I don't think so. I'd like to play and chat and relax. I figure the dinner itself will be intense enough. Maybe by the evening, we'll all be a little buzzed from the food and booze, so by nightfall we'll be ready to just play."

Martin asks what's going on.

"I didn't tell him. I didn't think it was my place," explains Tom to me.

Timothy hands out the beers. "On the house. The burgers will be about five minutes or so. Enjoy!"

I sip my beer. I tell Martin. A stranger. It's getting easier to tell my sorry tale. Why? Because it no longer feels like a sorry tale, not one for pity. I've spent so much time the last few days reliving the days in Europe and here, that I see how rich it all has been. I have no regrets. How magical is that?

Martin shakes his head and offers his heartfelt understanding. I tell them of all the dreams I've had, and making the scrapbook for Maggie, and of the trunk full of presents for my family and friends. Tom toasts my long, wonderful life. We clink glasses and start catching up in earnest.

An hour passes easily. Tom talks of the mountains in Southern Colorado and he describes the steep narrow dirt roads he drives in the hopes of spotting the wolves and coyotes he wants desperately to survive. The snowcapped peaks watch over him as he sits in the Landcruiser and drinks coffee from a thermos. Once a month, if that, he'll come across the tracks but has only seen three wolves so far, all last May.

Martin is a computer nerd, happy in his world of Internet consulting. The connection? They both live in log cabins up outside of Telluride. They go for a drink regularly and catch up then. They are obviously good friends despite a thirty year age difference.

I tell them of David and his home building. David is my young friend. I tell Tom about Paula, and how she lost Chris last year, so this party is for her as much as it is for me. A time for all the family to get together. He smiles sadly, knowingly. "Have you been publishing anything recently, Joey?"

"I haven't written more than one or two articles in the last year, not since the book came out, an anthology of my works on communities and political movements. I have some copies that came in the mail from the publisher. I plan on giving them away on Thursday. Want one? I'll sign it for you!"

Tom laughs and orders another round of drinks. Martin reminds us that we'll have to go after that. Tom grins and winks at me. "This is what we do. He has a timeframe for us. I like to keep drinking. And I order us an extra round before he notices, then he gives me a hard time, I feel bad for three seconds, and then we do it all again the following week!"

Martin laughs and admits he doesn't know why he bothers to keep on time with Tom around. Impossible to do with such an old man!

We drink our beers in front of the fire. Warmed and sated, we leave an hour later.

At home alone again, I decide to take Fred for a walk with me. The cats aren't impressed with the snow. I dress up in hat and scarf, and layers of shirts and the big green coat. We head outside. Fred has a puppy moment and runs with his nose in the snow, a snowplow. He stops near the gate and shakes his head. I laugh at his childlike expressions. I walk slowly. I'm full of beer.

The sun is partially hidden but still catches the snowflakes on the junipers. What a beautiful day. Tom is on his way to Maggie's. Martin will be back next weekend. Charlie will be here soon. Mike arrives tomorrow. I'm a little anxious about seeing him. I can only hope he understands now. And that he forgives me.

I think I'll make my favorite dinner of chicken and chile soup. With fresh tortillas warming on the stove. Not bad. I can do that.

I walk and talk to Fred. He can't hear me, but I like the sound of my own voice. It echoes through the arroyo. The temperature is dropping fast. More snow is predicted. It will indeed be a white Thanksgiving. Paula is coming over in the morning. She has been busy cooking, she told me on the phone, making pies and cakes and a surprise, a treat from my travels especially for the two of us. She won't tell me what! Oh, well. She's good at keeping secrets.

As am I.

Chapter Thirty-Nine

I'd felt sick to my stomach that day, waiting for Kat once again.

We'd stepped back into this incredible affair for almost a year. I'd come back from Russia with her, and I continued writing, but from living in New Mexico, instead of in Germany. I'd settled back into the small town life I knew so well. Kat would show up late at night to find me in bed. At fifty-years-old, I'd expected to be over her. But I wasn't. I was addicted. And so was she.

Still her terms though. When no one's looking.

I drank down yet another coffee. I paced. I waited. I waited for Kat. She had promised to meet me at the Flying Star Café on Central. It was one of the trendiest and most anonymous cafés for us. The university crowd filled the booths. I had a table for us out in the back room, with a newspaper, *El Pais*, to keep me patient. Waiting always put me in a bad mood. Kat knew that. I strode outside and smoked. I kept trying to quit but it never stuck. I smoked another.

Inside once again, and pretending to read, the noise was starting to get on my nerves when I saw her pull up and park out front. She looked through the window and waved. In she came. She was so striking. At forty-nine, she was unbelievably beautiful to me. I noticed quite a few heads turn to watch her as she came up to the table and kissed me on the lips, deeply, claiming what's hers. I could never resist. My eyes lit up and we sat down on the same bench. Her hands reached under the table and grabbed me.

"Mine!" she whispered in my ear and then bit me. "Did you find us a room?"

I laughed. "Needy today, are you, Kat?"

She squeezed me and replied that maybe we both were. I told her about paying for a room at the motel up the road, the one with the cowboy-style wooden framed beds and huge bathtubs.

"I know the one you mean. It's about three blocks away from the new Italian restaurant on the right. Did you want to eat here beforehand? I'm ravenous!" and she moved away from me. "Let me get a menu. Want more coffee, Joey?"

I watched her cross the room, oblivious of the appreciative glances from both men and women. She wore her jacket loose and I'd noticed an almost sheer slip covering her jeans, with the slight outline of a black bra peeking out above. I held my breath. This was going to be an interesting night. We had taken time apart while William was in town. A few weeks felt like an age to me. But then he never left on that job assignment as we'd hoped. So here we were. About to spend a night in one of the sleaziest motels on Central, a busy main through-way for the semi-trucks and buses crossing east to west in Albuquerque. I craved her. I'd missed her. And by her entrance, I knew she'd missed my touch.

I had another coffee; I knew I'd need the caffeine to keep my strength up. Kat was flirting outrageously, hungry for me. I laughed out loud with her suddenly innocent demeanor when the waiter brought the tray of food to us. We ate our burgers and salads. Fast. And then we left.

We drove her truck up the road and parked next to mine in the front lot by the office. The roads were busy even though the rush hour had passed. I took her to the room and unlocked the door. She pulled me inside. I'd barely closed the door before taking her against the wall. She held me fast. She used me as I used her. No talking needed. After almost thirty years as lovers, I knew what to do. And so did she. The strength of her need for me shattered the self-control I'd been hiding, and I cried when I came. Kat stroked my face gently and lay me down beside her, saying nothing.

In the morning, we were both broken. Exhausted physically and emotionally. We'd spent the night in and out of bed, ordering pizza and cokes from the new place nearby. We'd eaten in the bath. She'd washed my scruffy red hair and massaged my shoulders. We'd fucked in the shower. We'd talked as we lay in the sheets under neon lights from outside. I'd made her laugh till she snorted. She'd teased me until I held her down and tickled her speechless.

Outside, once the room was locked and paid for, we started to fight. Or rather, I started to fight. "Why not, Kat? Why can't you just love me? Be with me?"

"I can't. I never promised you I would, did I, Joey?"

I shook her hand off my arm. "But why can't you tell our friends you love me? Want to be with me? Why are you still with that prick, William?"

"There's nothing going on between you and me, no more than this. I keep telling you that. This is all it is."

"What? Sex? That's all?"

"Yes, and it's not enough for me to lose my home with William."

She was blunt, harsh and the chill in her eyes killed me. "Just let it go. Let it be what it is." She continued. "It's not like some regular relationship, is it? It never has been. And I never said it would be."

"So what if we've done it differently! I know you adore me, want me, and can't get enough of me. Last night says it all. Doesn't it?"

The traffic roared past, the early morning rush to get to work. I could hardly hear her, but I kept pushing her, provoking her to more and more callousness.

"Great sex isn't enough for me, Joey."

177

I'd wanted to shake her, get the truth out of her, the other truth, the kind I wanted to hear. "Come home with me, Kat. Be with me. I need you."

"No. I can't. And you know it. I've been honest all along. We're not together. And we never really have been."

"What about our home in Taos? Or coming to me in Spain? Guatemala? Here? What the fuck, Kat? Does it mean nothing to you? Do I mean nothing to you?"

"It's an affair. That's all. And I like it as it is. If you can't do this anymore, just say so."

We stared hard. My breath was shallow. The trucks raced past. I needed to scream. Or to kiss her. I didn't know which.

"Stop lying to me, Kat."

"I'm not lying. I love you." Kat stood in front of me with her arms crossed. She started to cry in frustration. "But you still don't understand me, do you?"

"No. Apparently not." And then I lost it. I completely lost it on her. Yelling at her and shoving her.

"I'm sick of it! I'm fucking sick of these lies! I can't take any more. I can't take it. I hate you! I hate you! I wish you'd just leave me alone." I stared at her one last time. "Goodbye, Kat."

And I stepped out in front of a semi.

Chapter Forty

I'd woken up screaming.

Screaming on and on. Flashing lights. Taste of metal. The smell of exhaust. Gravel in my mouth. Glass underneath. Sirens drowning out the voices of the medics. I heard but didn't understand. I watched Kat being taken away by two police officers. I watched the ravens watching me. And I kept on screaming. Too much pain. I faded out.

I have such vague memories of that day in Albuquerque. I do remember waking for the first time in intensive care. I was strapped to the bed, tubes everywhere. My arm lay limp at my side. A protective tent covered my numb legs. I knew no one.

I heard later that they first thought that Kat had pushed me deliberately. The cleaner at the motel stood up for her and swore she saw me jump out into the street. The truck driver couldn't remember anything from that day. He couldn't say either way. And I didn't speak. For six months, I didn't speak. Neither in the regular hospital, nor afterwards when I was back in the psych ward.

I spent six months walking with crutches, silent. Even in my own head, there was only silence. I stayed in the hospital, learning to walk again. Crutches. Then with a walking cane. My face was torn up and now scarred. Ribs were broken but healing. I'd shattered, well, pulverized the bones in my right arm and ankle. They rebuilt me with pins, metal, needle and thread. I'd been 'lucky,' they told me. Every day I had physiotherapy. Every day I had individual and group therapy. Finally, they got through to me. And I talked. And they listened.

The psychiatrist listened. The social worker listened.

Paula did her best, but she couldn't do much for me this time. Maggie helped as she could. They both kept the story from the family and told them I had gone to Europe for another book project.

"Joey will be in touch," Paula had told Mike; she'd given him Jimmy, my dog, (by then, he was our dog, I guess), the old truck and the home in Madrid, but only after boxing up any signs of Kat, hiding the boots, statue, and books.

I talked. The police returned. All charges against Kat were dismissed, and she was finally and fully removed from any suspicion. I didn't know what she did next, or where she went. Paula refused to talk about Kat. Maggie shook her head helplessly.

Upon my leaving after a year inside, the social worker extracted a promise from me: No contact with Kat.

I took a plane to Britain. And I stayed there for ten years before moving back to New Mexico with Eleanor at my side.

Chapter Forty-One

Paula pulls up outside and takes me out of my thoughts, not the prettiest ones. I truly am facing my demons. And now I get to face my friend. Paula climbs out of her Subaru with two bags, some pans and a milk jug, the old style, thick, heavy and opaque. She catches my eye and grins.

"Do I have treats for us today!" she walks toward me and passes the newspaper, a bag, and the pans, and gives me a quick peck on the cheek. We head straight toward the kitchen table and she unloads my arms, and then her own bag.

"I hope you're hungry, Joey. I figured we'd get some alone time this morning before everyone arrives. Mike's coming over tomorrow. Sam, too. I'm not sure about her daughter and the children; she'd said something about taking them into Madrid for a few hours. Anyway, how are you?"

"Sorta shaky, but doing well. No more falling over. Too many memories, though. It's driving me a bit nuts, all these voices in my head! I can't hear myself talk to Fred!"

"Who were you thinking about when I pulled up? You looked sad but happy, if you know what I mean. It wasn't Kat, I'd guess." And she laughs to soften the truth of her words.

I sit down with the scrapbook and show her what I've been working on.

"Oh, Joey, it's beautiful. What are you going to do with it?" and Paula flicks through each page slowly and appreciatively.

"Give it to Maggie. It's much of the stuff I sent her and that she made for me whenever I was away. Even the first painting she gave me that night I got to Madrid, when she was three. Isn't that crazy? Funny little monkey girl she was."

Paula smiles sweetly as she keeps reading and looking at the now full book before her. She stands back up.

"I have a taste for you from Spain. I made them myself last night. Want some churros and hot chocolate?"

"Really! Oh, my God, Paula. I'd love some." And I start going through her bags. She slaps me away.

"Sit down and behave yourself! I'll take care of it. Now, sit down, Joey. Tell me about the things you're remembering."

"Well, Kat, of course. And Eleanor. She was a constant friend for me when I lived in Wales. Living with her in London taught me so much, too. And now I feel bad about bringing her here, away from her daughter and son, but..."

"But, she loved you dearly. And you know it. Don't feel guilty. Didn't she strike you as someone who did what she wanted? I thought of her as being pretty tough. That's why I didn't worry about her being with you."

I look up, surprised. "Really? You thought I took that much work?"

"Well, yes." And now Paula looks surprised. "You don't? You had such a shitty time there, not just anyone could've held up so well."

"Suppose so. That's the great thing about old friends, eh? No holds barred with you!"

Paula grins and hands me a mug of Spanish-style thick hot chocolate. She pours herself a mug. And then out comes a warm dish of churros. She lays them on the table and sits down with me.

"You've never made these before, have you?"

"Are you trying to tell me something? Think I got them wrong?"

"Hell, no!" I dunk one in the mug and out it comes dripping in pure cocoa. I put it into my mouth eagerly and suck on the chocolate like a ten-year-old. "This is a nutritional orgasm!"

"Joey!" and she does exactly the same, giggling and eating more. We start to compete again. Food fight, but without the mess. Food race? Would that be more accurate? Four each and then I give up. I can't take anymore. Three lie on the plate.

"Dare you," I challenge her.

She chokes on her drink and shakes her head helplessly. "No chance. Let's save them for David. He's never tried them, has he?"

"I doubt it. And I know I'm stuffed."

I move the plate to her side of the table. She pushes it back to me. I stand and put it on the counter behind her. We sip the rest of the chocolate. And then I bring us both water, huge glasses of water. "What a way to start my diet!"

"Hah, hah. I'm the one who's sticking around. I'll be all fat by the time you give up on this life. So what were you thinking about, really?"

I sit back down after stoking the fire. I look around the cabin. The walls are plastered and painted in warm colors, oranges and reds and golds. The wood is blue and green, mostly. Eleanor did the tile work across the kitchen counters and in the shower to the right of me.

"Remember when I brought her back here the first time in when we were all turning sixty? You two took to each other, to the point of shutting me outside in order to talk more freely! Chris and I went to the tavern to see some cover band or other. I was terrified of bumping into Kat on my own. I didn't know what to say to her. But, anyway, this home was hers. Eleanor's. These tiles she found for us in Taos. The rainbow paints she gathered from the neighbors in Cerrillos, at one of the yard sales. We both looked for months for the right flooring. She wanted Saltillo tile. I wanted wood." Paula and I instinctively look down at the Saltillo tiles and laugh.

"Yep, she had a soft touch that got you to do what she wanted!" Paula teases gently. She had been so happy to see my love for Eleanor deepen over the years. I didn't even know what was going on. I'd never loved like that before. Partners. Friends. Family. Two years ago she passed on, a sudden death in her sleep, next to me, at home. I'd held her in my sleep, breathing together. But then, I'd woken to her cold body. And I'd called Paula.

I'd let Eleanor go fairly easily. I didn't break down. I walked the mountains around us. I walked our dogs. I fed the cats. I finished the house and counted my blessings. She loved me. I loved her. Simple as that. No drama. No earthquakes, but a sweet gentle love we shared in our later years. Good company. A good woman. I miss her.

I talk to Paula of how I'd tried to recover a sense of purpose when I'd moved to Britain. A reason to live fully. I describe the walks I took in the hills of Southwest Wales. And how I wrote in my cottage by the sea, going out occasionally to have one beer with the locals in Rhossili. I walked, meditated, grew food and wrote.

"And then I met Eleanor. I bumped into her so much that we become good friends within days. I doubt I'd have stayed in Wales for so long, gone to London, or even come back to New Mexico without her suggesting it. Huh! I hadn't realized at the time but yeah, that lady of mine sure did get me to do what she wanted. She tricked me! I think she just wanted to see what these mountains were like!"

"She took her own sweet time with you, that's for sure. How long before you moved out of your bachelor pad in the country?"

"You mean my move to London? Four years, I think, something like that. It was around the end of the '90s, I remember all the end of the world articles in the papers. Anyway, before that, I came to see her once a month in the city. She came down to me on the academic holidays, with piles of essays to correct. We'd both sit at my huge table, with papers spread out, silently working on our projects. I'd look up and watch her writing carefully to her students, her pen behind her ear when she was thinking to herself." I shake my head softly.

Paula goes over to the cats, who are sprawling on the bed as usual. "David tells me he's planning on taking care of Fred and these guys. I'm glad."

"Me, too. He's a good kid. Grandson. And you were a great mom to them, Paula. I know you think you failed Charlie, but he's good. He's doing well in California. And Mike, too. He's happy in Chicago. Or so Maggie tells me."

"Have you talked to Mike yet?" she asks me.

'Nope. I'm waiting for him to show up and then I'll know what to say."

"Want to talk about it?"

"Not really. Can you wait? I'll tell you afterwards, promise."

She nods and then scratches two happy bellies. Fred ambles over to me and sits and stares at the churros on the counter. "Can I give him some?"

"A little bit. It'll be too rich for the old fella. A little should be fine."

She stretches out on my bed and tells the ceiling that she talked to Charlie a few nights before. "And we had a great talk. The first in ages. He described his work that day, recreating a wooden and metal spiral staircase. I told him why I'd asked everyone to come back this Thanksgiving. About your limited time with us. And how much it meant to me to know he was coming out here. He took a few minutes. Sad. He's always looked up to you, Joey. And then he said he had something to tell me. He came out. And I mean the gay kind." She sits up. "How did I not know?" She looks at me, stares at me, and I look down at Fred and scratch his ears. "You knew! You little shit, you knew!"

I shrug. "Maybe!" and then I grin widely.

"You knew my son is gay, and you didn't tell me? Why not?" and she throws a pillow at me.

"It wasn't my place to, was it? He'd asked me to keep the secret for him."

Ah, that silences us both. She has kept quiet on my behalf. And I stood there for her kids when they needed someone to talk to. She understands. I know she does.

And I smirk. "He's so gay!"

"Joey!"

"Well, he is! When you think about it, Paula. All that remodeling and those fancy jobs he gets in San Francisco. That and not having any girl-friends when he comes to visit us, how could you not know?"

She tells me that Charlie is bringing someone home with him.

"He wants us to meet Robert. An artist and 'close' friend. Do you think it's a boyfriend?"

And now I can't stop shaking with laughter, slapping my knees and teasing her. "Oh, yes! Perfect! It won't be all about me. I'm so gay, and I mean I'm happy, that kind!"

Paula watches me, trying hard to keep a straight face, so to speak.

"Right. Well. I told Charlie that they can stay with me, in your old studio and he loved the idea. He asked if I had any copies of your books lying around. Do you?"

That stops me. "Actually, I do! I have six copies left, and I was going to give them to the guys on Thursday. I have some other presents for them, too."

"Like what?"

I stand up slowly and walk to the woodstove. I pick up a few cedar logs and shove them inside. "The Will we can talk about later. But for now, I had a painting for Charlie. My old tools from the '60s for Mike. The scrap-book for Maggie."

"And for me?" Paula grins. "What about me?"

I shake my head, "Not telling! You have to wait, Miss Paula."

Paula throws the other pillow at me. And you can guess how I let her get away with that, can't you?

A few hours later, we both drift off, sitting in front of the fire. I hadn't told her what she was getting. Probably because I don't know what to give her. What can I give her? Oh, hell. Think fast. I have less than twenty-four hours. I fall asleep.

Chapter Forty-Two

I dream of Mike, and when I last saw him. Such a painful moment for the both of us.

Betrayal filled his eyes. And all because he'd seen my birth certificate years before. He'd found it that second time he'd been living at my place in Madrid, in the '90s. He'd ended up cleaning away the rest of my things after my disappearance to Wales. I'd written to let him know the home was his, and I sent him the deeds signed over in his name.

Mike was amazed. But then he cut me out of his life. Not that I knew why at the time. He'd finally told me the reason shortly after Eleanor died. Two years ago. The day he'd showed up out of the blue, after the funeral.

He came to me; he drove up to the home I'm in now. I'd been sitting in the pink rocking chair. I'd been watching the two ravens in the juniper near the kitchen window. I missed Eleanor. Sad. Deeply and quietly sad that afternoon. I saw Mike. And I was glad for the company.

Mike climbed out of his Chevy and walked slowly up to the house. "Hey, Uncle Joey."

"Uncle? You never call me that anymore!" I looked up at him, taken aback by the words as much as the tone.

"Want to know why?" He came up the steps. "Want to know why you never heard me say it after you gave me the house? Or when you and Eleanor showed up a decade later?"

"Sure. Come on in. I have some beers, if you want one."

I opened the door and Mike followed me in. He closed it softly, but I sensed something was amiss. I turned back to him and he was crying in rage, his face was bright, shiny and tear-soaked.

"Mike. What's wrong?" I stepped closer and reached out to him but he pushed me away. And then he spat out, "Or should I call you Aunty Josephine?"

I sat down. My knees gave way. "Mike, I can explain…"

"No, you can't. You lied to me, all those years when I was a little kid, calling you Uncle. And you're not. Nothing like it. You're a fucking woman and you've been lying to me, to all of us, for how long? Our whole lives! MY WHOLE LIFE!" and he slammed out of the house and ran to his truck.

Chapter Forty-Three

Maggie unloads her Honda with some of my favorite familiar faces. I'm tired after talking all day yesterday with Paula. I shake myself as I look out the window. Remember, this is for me. Paula is home probably cooking up a storm, knowing her. And I'm grumpy about not having time to myself? Funny, eh? I'll have time soon enough. This might be the last time I see Samantha and her family. Any of them. My heart breaks another fraction.

I stand up to welcome them to my home.

Maggie has her arms full of bags. And here is Sam, and Tom's come with her. Two young girls step out of the back doors. The granddaughters are ten and thirteen by the looks of it. Samantha has filled out and has become the archetypal grandmother, with grey hair up in a bun, scarves wrapped around her shoulders, and she still has the lightness of smiles that lights her face when she sees me on the front porch.

David comes out from his camper. Sam waves the kids in his direction and I see the older girl blush. They run over to him and he takes them into the camper with Fred following along. The cats sit next to me, sharing the front door and then they stroll back toward the bed again.

I wait for Maggie and Sam to walk up to me. I hold them both. We all tear up slightly, but I try to keep it light. I must be worn out if I'm crying so easily. Sam recovers quickly and steps inside my home. I hear a sigh of recognition. "It's just like our home in Panajachel. Oh, Joey, it has the same feeling! How wonderful. And you and Eleanor made this together, didn't you? You'd told me, but I didn't know you'd make it like this, so comfortable and simple and colorful! I taught you well!"

Maggie chuckles. "I think my mom claims that one!"

"Hey, now, I'm still in the room, you know! And anyway, I taught myself!" at which they look at each other and cackle in unison.

I close the door behind us and put the kettle on. I pull out David's oatmeal cookies and Paula's churros and place them all on the table. Sam and Maggie chat about the plans for the next day. I'm told that as the guest of honor, I'm having a chauffeur come pick me up at 11:00 in the morning. Paula has told them that I'm to be ready with my things by 10:30 at the latest. Hmm. I grin though at their rendition of who arrived and when. It sounds like everyone's made it in time before the storm strikes.

"Five inches of snow is expected tonight! Isn't that crazy?"

"I'm not ready for this, but the grandkids can't wait. We just don't get weather like this in Bisbee. Up in Flagstaff when we visit the family, but not at home."

Maggie tells of the first time she remembers it snowed for a Thanksgiving. She was four and she thought I'd made it snow just for her! And when her big brothers teased her, she went crying to Paula, but she'd still believed I had magic up my sleeves.

"I'd forgotten about that! You loved the crayon trick, too."

Sam laughs. "You taught her that one, too? I remember all the girls in Pana loved that one. Silly weren't you?"

"Well, I'm a bit slower with the tricks up my sleeves these days, but you should see Paula and me when we're alone. Talk about being foolish! Trust me, she's just as silly as ever!"

Tom is perched against the counter, pouring out the water into the teapot. "Are you ready for the big day tomorrow?"

"Yeah! I'm a little overwhelmed, but I want to see everyone together. So this is perfect, eh? All of us in a snow storm together! I love it."

And then I hear another truck heading this way. Mike pulls up in a smart Toyota. He grins as he steps out. He waves to me, and he is full of the life and joy I'd been missing in our friendship. He's forgiven me. He walks over to me, very much a fit and healthy man in his late forties. He catches me in a bear hug. He's strong, too! Before I can protest, he whispers so I only I can hear him.

"Sorry."

"Oh, Mike. Mike. Mike. Welcome back."

I kiss him quickly on the cheek. He turns to the others. He looks for a second before saying, "Hey there, Samantha! Tom! I didn't recognize you both to start with. Joey, I came over because Mom, Katie, Charlie and Robert went to the Mine Shaft. Want to come with us? Start a day early?"

Tom pours the tea down the drain. And that is that. We round up the kids and pile into Maggie's car and Mike's truck. He and I drive alone.

We need time together.

Mike drives onto Highway 14 and heads toward Madrid, following the steep hill down into the valley. The road drops off to the right of us. The snow is coming down much faster now and the windshield wipers are clearing the way for us. Maggie drives super carefully. I mean slowly. Think tortoise.

"I hope she's not my driver tomorrow!" I mutter.

Mike laughs and then passes her. "I haven't told anyone, by the way. Not my place."

"Thanks. Do you want me to tell them?"

"Yes, but it's really your choice, isn't it?"

"True. Okay, I'll think about it when you buy the first round!"

Mike pulls up to the bar and grins. "Deal! What do you want?"

Chapter Forty-Four

Inside, the fire is raging and it's a full house. Timothy has set us up at the big round table by the heat. The radio is playing in the background but the first impression is of a crowded house party, with everyone talking over each other. I smile. This is home. A home away from home. Mike steps around me and kisses his girlfriend before bringing her over to say hello to me.

Katie gives me a hug, saying, "So you're Joey, who's given him such a hard time, huh? Imagine letting him stay in that house of yours for all those years! No wonder he fixed up my place within the first six months of us dating. He couldn't help himself and he said it's all your fault!" and Mike shrugs, both proud and embarrassed.

He pulls out a chair for me next to Paula. She has a white wine, as usual. Timothy arrives with a pint of Santa Fe Pale Ale for me. He turns to the rest of the table and writes down orders for food and drinks. For the eleven of us.

Charlie grins at me, reaches over and shakes my hand before introducing me to Robert. Charlie is tanned and good-looking just like his father was, the dark brown eyes have a twinkle of lightness that I always loved to see. For a fifty-one-year-old, his hair is still thick, cut very short and his face shows little sign of wear. Robert is the same height but more average-looking, with a short goatee, tidily trimmed light brown hair and a wide smile. They are both dressed in jeans and obviously new western-style shirts under thick winter coats. They are both very much city folk now, and Charlie is quite the contrast to the scruffy little boy I knew. I say just that and Robert laughs and leans in. "Oh really? Do tell!"

And so, with a little encouragement, I tell of my first impressions when I arrived in Madrid, 1967. How I dropped my motorcycle on the dirt road that night after a few too many drinks in Santa Fe. I described Maggie's entrance in her big brother's hand-me-downs.

"I couldn't get in them now," she jokes. And everyone looks between Maggie with her matronly full figure and Mike's fit and constantly energetic body. His light reddish hair is tied back into a ponytail and he beams in pride as he flexes his muscles.

"He works out three times a week," whispers Katie for all to hear.

"And he never had kids, like I did!" offers Maggie in her own defense.

"I keep trying to, what, most nights, right, Katie?" and we all turn to see Katie turn beetroot red.

"Nice weather! How much snow do you think we'll get?" asks Paula, picking up her wine glass.

We all groan at the attempt to distract. But heh, Katie's new; we should pick on someone else! David, perhaps?

"Where's Jamie today?" I ask.

He grins and groans. "My turn?"

I smile sweetly and drink my beer. "Yep. Tell us about you and Jamie!"

"I can do that myself!" and Jamie sits on his lap, much to his obvious discomfort in front of his mom. "What did you want to know?"

And everyone laughs, as it's now David's turn to blush.

I watch my best friend. Paula beams when she looks around the table. Her family. My family. The banter continues and the beers flow.

Chapter Forty-Five

"A toast!"

"Yes, a toast!" cries out Maggie.

Mike looks over Katie's head to me, a shrug. No words needed. I nod.

"I have a toast. It's a short one. But I have a feeling we'll be talking about it for a while to come. Are you ready?"

Paula sits up, unsure of what's up. Charlie smiles encouragingly. Robert reaches over and I can tell they are holding hands under the table. Mike and Katie cuddle. He watches me intently. The girls wander off to the porch—they don't know me. Sam has tears in her eyes. The table is quiet. I'm ready. David and Jamie pull up two more chairs.

"Some of you know why we asked you to come back this year. Some of you don't. I've had an amazing life, and I'm so thankful, blessed to know each of you. A huge part of my life came with one or more of you at my side. Paula. You are the family, the sister I wished for. You are everything to me. This party is for you, too. And for Chris and for Eleanor who are no longer at the table with us. But Paula, I reckon we're lucky. This is our family. Maggie, Charlie, Mike, you are my beloved nephews and niece. All of you are such good friends to me. David. Sam. Tom." I pause. I need to take a breath. I sip some water. "I have bad news for you, or not so bad, really, I've made my peace with it. I hope you can, too. I'm going away. Not to Europe this time. I don't know where. But I'm okay with that. I have a couple of months left. It's cancer."

I stop a moment. All around the room, I notice the love and laughter that enriches this unique community. I turn back and continue with a soft smile for these sad, smiling and teary-eyed familiar faces. "Let's enjoy the next few days together, and know that I love you dearly. And before I leave you all, I wanted to say, let's have no more secrets, okay? I've kept too many secrets. And I've asked some of you to keep quiet and tell my lies, the ones I'd made in the name of love.

"A few of you know this last secret of mine. My full name is Josephine Andrews. I'm, well, I'm not the man you thought I was – so to speak! I just never really felt like a Josephine. Joey suits me much better. Right? Anyway, thanks for just taking me as I am. I hope this isn't too much of a shock all at once. So, let's just drink a toast to friends and family, one and the same!"

Incomprehension. Knowing smiles. And then everyone is talking at once. A riot of jokes and questions drowns out the rest of the bar. I grin and down my beer.

"I knew it!" shouts Tom. "I always thought you were a sissy! Too much of a sensitive hippy boy! Well, that explains why you and Sam never had kids together!"

Sam swats him lightly on the shoulder. "I couldn't tell you—it was best you didn't know, Tom. We'd have had too much to hide, what with your work putting us on the line anyway, right?"

Tom nods and I see them start talking quietly between them, Sam smiles sweetly at me, and mouthed words of love I know we share.

"What other secrets do you have, Joey?" Charlie grins as Robert suddenly blurts out,

"We have one! We're getting married!"

"Really? How? I mean…" and Paula stops, all flustered. She looks at them both, and reaches over to kiss her boy on the cheek and shake Robert's hand.

"It's okay, Mom. We're not doing this officially, but well, we want to make it public, since we've been together for three years now. No more hiding, right, Robert?" They toast each other and turn back to the topic at hand.

"Cancer. And you're a gender queer! Quite a first impression you're making on me," offers Robert with an open smile. The table goes quiet for a moment.

"Yep, welcome to the family!" I raise my glass to him with a grin.

And then there is a round of deep freeing laughter, all chatting to each other across the huge table, glasses clinking. I see hugs, and tears and questions and champagne flowing and looks of surprise and stories and mistakes and honesty and more jokes and brotherly teasing and affection and all I can think is, This is my family.

I turn to Mike, the one who needs to hear this the most. Katie wanders off.

David listens in, quiet, and I think stunned by all of this. He'd never guessed. "I feel like an idiot for not knowing," he mutters. Jamie hugs him tightly and whispers something I can't hear.

"I am sorry, David. I never meant to lie to you. I love you. I love all of you."

David looks over to his uncle with a question in his eyes. They nod and Mike talks for the both of them.

"That part I get." Mike can't help but ask, " But why be a man when you're not?"

"You have to know the whole story. In the '50s and '60s, people like me were killed; they beat us up all the time. Gays. Queers. Dykes. Butch bulldaggers, whatever the name given, we were never accepted. Only in the most liberal places, maybe, but even then… I grew up on a small island in Maine, and they hated me. And then I moved every few years as a teenager. One family sending me to the next. It was horrible, Mike. The kids at the schools beat me up because my dad had killed my mom."

"I didn't know that!" he turns to me, shocked. "When?"

"I was eight years old. Only your mom knew. Even Chris didn't. Anyway, they hated me for being a 'killer's kid' and then for how I dressed like a boy. I didn't have words for it. I don't know that I do now."

"Did you want to be a man? That's the part that still gets me. Why pretend?"

"It just happened. I wore men's loose work clothes because I liked them, still do. Girl clothes don't make any sense to me!"

Mike laughs. "Me, neither. Okay, so next question, don't you like being a woman?"

"I *am* a woman, and I never really denied it. No one asked! You see, I like working with my hands. I like writing. I love women. I wear men's clothes. As I got older and skinnier and scruffy in the '60s, people just figured I was a hippy boy. I never told them otherwise. It made things easier for me, that's all."

"Why not tell us?"

"When? There never seemed the right time. I'm sorry you found out like you did, but I'm not sorry for how I lived my life as a man. It worked for me. Still does. And it's not like I didn't get the girls! Or keep them!"

And now Mike snorts. "Hell, yeah, but look at the mess you got into with them!" he laughs again, but softly this time, a sweet sound that brings a smile to my heart. He carries on, saying, "I'm glad you've met Katie now." He glances over at me, and stands up. "I'm going to go find her. I don't want to lose her because of my crazy family!" He grins, "Do you need anything since I'm up?"

I shake my head.

Paula comes to me and holds me close. "You told!"

"I promised Mike, no more secrets. That was the last one. And speaking of which, I have a surprise for you."

"What is it? Is it my present?"

I laugh. "Yeah, good guess. You can have it tomorrow, I promise!" I'm fibbing. I still have no idea what to give her.

"I have a secret for *you*." Paula grins at me.

"You do? What?"

"I'll tell you later!" and she tickles me, and then heads off to the bathroom, laughing with Samantha as they weave in and out of all the tables and chairs.

Maggie comes up to me. "I never told anyone about that stuff, Joey. You know that, right?"

"I know, sweetheart. You kept your promises. Ever since that second time I was in hospital. We couldn't pretend anymore, could we?" And I hug her tightly to me. She tries not to cry but I feel her start to shake. "It's okay, Maggie."

"I have a secret I need to tell you." And she looks up at me, all teary-eyed.

"Okay. What's that?"

"I told."

I nod. "Yes?"

"Told Kat." She mutters quietly.

"Told her about the cancer?"

"No, I told her where you were. Every time she looked for you, I told her." And now Maggie has tears pouring off her sad little guilty face.

I try hard not to laugh when I tell her I knew. I'd guessed that many times over. "The postcards, right? You showed her the postcards?"

"Yeah, Mom told me I wasn't allowed to say anything. So I didn't. I pointed to the fridge."

I smile and hug her before telling her to relax, I don't mind. And that I'm probably happy she did tell Kat in her own way. She looks relieved. She sits back down.

I walk out onto the porch that overlooks the highway and a few galleries. David comes out and passes me a joint. He stands in front of the cameras to hide us. Jamie steps out and lights a cigarette. She leans against the wall and watches David and me smoke and chat. No questions, no comments from either of them. Just easy company. On the way back in, they both simply say thanks. And that is that.

Charlie goes to the band setting up and talks to the guitarist for a while. Robert watches before turning to Tom and Sam and asking how they know me. I listen in for a while. Paula sits back and nods in my direction. I smile. We know. We both know. I tip my glass and salute her. She throws her ice cube at me when no one watches. It hits my forehead with a clunk. She snorts and then pretends not to know what the commotion is about.

The table comes back together when the food appears. More drinks, more stories come out. I listen more than I talk. The conversations cover everything from everyone's travels, their art projects, favorite books, and even touch on questions of gender, sexuality and, of course, all kinds of illnesses.

I eat my enchiladas.

The band starts up. Charlie drags Robert up closer to watch. The dance floor fills. Paula sits back and watches her kids and our friends. I put another log on the fire. She has an evil knowing grin. I don't know why.

Then I notice someone is standing close to me on my left. I turn around and stare at a pair of black and red cowboy boots right next to me. I look up. Kat has cropped her hair to an inch or so, salt and pepper slowly pushing out all signs of the blackness I knew so well. Her face is tanned; the years have been kind to her. Her charcoal eyes pull me in once again.

"Come on, Joey, dance with me."

Kat holds out her hand and I reach for her instinctively. I can do nothing else. Even now.

Paula laughs behind us, clapping and crowing, "Surprise! Look who's come to see you again!"

The two women share a sweet knowing smile, and I look between them. They both grin oh-so-innocently. Kat is here. Paula must have told her. And Kat came back to me. She came back. Despite everything.

"Dance with me, Joey? I know that you don't really like country western music, but come dance with me. It's been a while. Or aren't you up for it? Too old these days?" Kat's eyes sparkle with a gentle challenge.

"Well, I think I can manage just one or two." I put down my drink and I stand up, ready to swing us both around, telling her just that.

Kat laughs, pulls me into a hug, and whispers, "I'm coming home with you. I'm staying this time." She holds me close.

"But for how long?" I can't help but ask, stepping back.

And Kat just shrugs, smiling widely, and says nothing.

I reach for her anyway.

Lightning Source UK Ltd.
Milton Keynes UK
04 October 2010

160725UK00003B/153/P